I0747235

PIPER'S PRICE

A DEBT COLLECTION NOVELLA

ANDREW GIVLER

AUTHOR'S NOTE

Piper's Price *takes place between* Soul Fraud *(Book One) and* Dandelion Audit *(Book Two) in the Debt Collection series, but it was written with the intent to be a starting point to experience the world of the series even if you haven't read the first book.*

Toward that end, the only spoilers that exist in this novella are thematic in nature. Everything you learn in this story are things you find out very quickly in Soul Fraud. *Knowing them ahead of time should not impact your ability to enjoy the series if you decide to give it a shot after reading this.*

—Andrew

PIPER'S PRICE

CHAPTER
ONE

I**T'S A TESTAMENT** to the sheer volume of bad choices I've made—or in some cases haven't made—that I found myself in a room full of corpses on an August afternoon. I didn't kill them, but that didn't make them smell any better. Even in paradise it gets hot in the summer. Granted, most people in SoCal would never call the Valley paradise. There are some nice houses, like this one that was full of bodies. But there's all that heat, and you have to deal with the 405 if you want to get anywhere cool.

My name is Matthew Carver. Four months ago, I was a pretty normal guy. Well, maybe not *normal*. If I'm keeping it a buck, I was a loser. Things were not going well. They're not going any better now, obviously—but they are going *differently*. On my twenty-fourth birthday, I was visited by a demon salesman. His name was Dan, and he came with the classic infernal offer. The one that goes something like this: "Yadda, yadda, get a perfect life for ten years, just sign over your soul." Back in ye olde days it might have been more appealing, but I have seen that TV show. I know it's a bad idea. So I declined the offer. But Dan was behind on his quota and faked my signature on the contract before running off.

At first I didn't think much of it, because I'm not a lunatic. Demons obviously weren't real; souls might not be either. There were a hundred rational explanations for what had just happened to me.

Then everything changed.

Ever since that demon ran off with my soul, there's been drama. Now I work for the Hunter, which is nice because he is very scary and protects me from my many enemies. But it also means that I end up in some really weird situations, like the one I was currently in. I'm not sure that a room of rotting corpses was an improvement over my old life, but it certainly wasn't boring.

Three people died in this room. It looked like they had all gone peacefully; each had a sort of serene expression on their face, as if they had been in the middle of something pleasant and simply expired. Somehow that made the scene even creepier.

My aforementioned boss, Orion—Nephilim, Constellation, and master of the Hunt—crouched in the center of the room, peering at the carnage with a practiced air. His solid black eyes were narrowed as he studied the tapestry of violence someone had left behind.

The Hunter is something of an artist when it comes to killing—as if that's not obvious from the sword that's always slung over his shoulder—he's been doing it for thousands of years. Someone was so impressed by his abilities that they made a billboard of stars in the night sky to honor him.

"What do you see?" Alex whispered softly from my left. I rolled my eyes and gave him a glare. Orion's pointed ears can hear an ant tie its shoes at a hundred yards. There's no way the Hunter hadn't heard that.

Alex is slightly taller than I am at six foot one. He's a Nephilim like Orion, which means that at some point in his family tree, someone was born to the union of a human and a demon. But Alex's DNA is more mortal than Orion's by a significant margin. His eyes have normal irises which are blue, though someone looking closely might notice that his ears are ever-so-slightly pointed. A natural affection for style and perfectly coiffed blond hair make him seem like a pretty boy, but he's handy in a fight. Two hundred years of practice will do that for you.

We're both technically the Hunter's squires, which mostly means that he asks us questions we don't know the answers to, then grunts in irritation when we get them wrong. Being practical underachievers, Alex and I have made a habit of sharing homework whenever we can, despite the fact that we're both competing at all times to be Squire of the Month. It's not a good system, but it's all we got.

THERE'S NO POINT IN DOING IT WHEN THE BIG GUY IS RIGHT IN FRONT OF US, I tried to shout at my friend with my eyes. It's the only method of communication quiet enough that Orion can't hear. Alex shrugged at my irritation and glanced back at the room.

Ignoring my friend, I turned my attention back to the carnage too. He was right that Orion was going to start asking us
questions any second now—

"Time of death?" the Hunter grunted without looking at us.

"Two days ago," I replied after taking a deep sniff and wish-
ing I hadn't.

"Be more specific."

"Thirty-six hours," I guessed. How in the world was I supposed to know how long it had been? I hadn't really graduated
from college, and I was an *English major*. I can spell *death* but
not explain it. That's for the STEM students.

"Wrong."

"Thirty-two," Alex piped up, giving me an apologetic shrug.

"These two were thirty-one." Orion sighed in mild disap-
pointment.

"How?" I demanded, knowing the answer would be even
more frustrating than not knowing.

The Hunter raised a long finger and tapped his nose, still
staring at the scene before him. "It's in the balance of rot against
the other scents of the room." I rolled my eyes. Of course he
could smell decay down to the hour. Alex shifted next to me,
uncomfortable with the direct comparison of Orion's capabili-
ties against his.

It wasn't his fault; it was literally genetics. Orion's supernatural olfactory glands are just one of the lovely perks he gets for
being a demigod, or pretty dang close to one. The concentration
of demonic DNA that runs in his veins makes him an immortal.
He's not a man, he's something more.

"What do you mean these two? What about him?" I asked,
pointing to the man in the center.

"Twenty-nine hours," Orion answered without hesitation. "Why the difference?"

"I do not know." The Hunter was silent for a moment, staring at something I couldn't see. Then the moment was gone, and he was back on the move. "What killed them?" Orion asked, taking control of the questions again, rising from his crouch. He's an intense guy, but he's also my friend. He's saved my life too many times not to be.

"Poison?" I guessed, eyeing the corpses once more. There weren't any open wounds that I could see.

"Gas?" Alex offered, clearly following the same line of logic as me. Some sort of carbon monoxide poisoning might have put this party to sleep before any of them even knew anything was wrong.

That would be too easy an answer. The Hunter only shook his head, his black gaze still fixed on the victims in front of us. "You're missing something important," he chided absentmindedly. Whatever he had noticed was distracting him from being disappointed in us.

Frustrated with myself, I ran my gaze over the three corpses again, trying to use a more critical eye. In the last four months, I've seen enough bodies that they don't make me want to puke anymore, but I still wasn't wholly comfortable hanging around death like this. It's creepy.

There seemed to be little rhyme or reason to the bodies. They were all adults; one woman was in her mid-twenties, the second perhaps her early forties, and the man had gray in his hair. None of them looked related. They just seemed like a random collection of people off the streets. If I was shown these people in a police lineup, I'd have no reason to suspect that they knew each other, let alone died together.

A figure shifted uncomfortably in the entryway and cleared his throat. "Is this the best use of our time?" the man asked nervously. I glanced over my shoulder to eye the lawyer. He was dressed in a simple black suit and had slick black hair to match. His name was Driscoll, and he knew Orion somehow. Well, I knew how he knew Orion. The pointy ears were a dead giveaway. He was some sort of supernatural lawyer—

Oh.

My neck whipped back around to the bodies so fast that for a second, I saw different kind of stars. My heart began to race as my gaze flipped from one body to the next. By the third one, I knew what connected them. It was the same thing that everyone in this room but me had in common.

"They're all Nephilim," I breathed in horror. Alex let out a small sigh of frustration that he'd missed it.

"They're all Nephilim," Orion agreed, his abyss-filled eyes still taking in the corpses of his cousins. "You were right to call me first, Driscoll."

"Of course," the nervous lawyer agreed. "But this is too many bodies to hide from the mortal police. They will find this, and the sooner we report it, the less danger we will be in."

"We're already in danger," Orion mused, crouch-walking another step toward the bodies. A chill ran down my spine at the Hunter's words, and I traded a knowing look with Alex. Orion tends to be pretty hard to intimidate. I've seen him face down high-ranking demons without even blinking. For him to admit there was danger present was unheard of. The ruby in the hilt of his sword winked at me over his shoulder, as if it were secretly thrilled at the news.

"Pardon?" Driscoll breathed, clearly as surprised as we squires were.

"I knew Dardan." Orion gestured at the center Nephilim, the one who'd died last. "He was very strong." I took that as a delicate way of saying Dardan had a hefty dose of demon blood in his veins.

"What could take out all these Nephilim at once, especially one like him?" I demanded. How do you sneak up on someone who has the hearing of a bat?

Orion didn't answer. Moving with intense purpose, he rose and walked toward Dardan. The man's eyes were closed, and there was a faint smile on his face. He looked like he might be asleep—if you ignored the mild bloating and smell.

Slowly, the Hunter reached two of his fingers into the front pocket of the man's button-down shirt and drew out a black business card. At first glance, it seemed to be blank, but when Orion flipped it over, I saw a logo. It was a simple line drawing of a rock set in the middle of the sea and etched in gold.

The Hunter stared at it for a long moment, frozen, as if the very atoms of his body had ceased their vibrations. It was a sign of shock from immortals such as him.

"What is it?" Alex ventured after a moment.

"Someone taking responsibility." Orion's tone was as black as the card in his hand.

"Who?" I asked. The Hunter was silent for another long moment, staring at the logo in front of him. He looked like he had just seen a ghost, which, given the number of fresh bodies in the room, wouldn't be surprising.

"Someone I killed centuries ago," Orion answered at last.

Oh boy.

THE HUNT DIDN'T stay long after Orion found the card of his long-dead enemy. We packed up in Alex's beat-up white minivan and hit the road right after Orion gave Driscoll his blessing to report the bodies to the police. The nervous lawyer had promised to take care of it and hadn't asked any more questions.

I was riding shotgun as we made our way onto the parking lot that is the 405 South after 3 p.m. on a weekday. Orion sat behind me, brooding in the captain's chair of the second row. I'm never quite sure if he insists on riding back there because there's more legroom or as a power thing. Could be both.

There was a tense silence as we sat in bumper-to-bumper

traffic, waiting for our boss to explain who the card was from. The 405 is more a pressure cooker than a highway, and I was feeling its effect. I saw a news report recently that said it is the most congested freeway in the United States. I've never lived outside LA, so I don't technically have a frame of reference, but I believe it.

After thirty minutes of being stonewalled from the inside and the outside of the car, I couldn't take it anymore. Orion is very scary, but in the way that a Doberman is scary. I knew this dog, so some of the myth had faded for me.

"Well?" I demanded, turning in my seat to glare over my shoulder at our boss. "Are you gonna tell us who the card is from, or do we have to deal with another ninety minutes of your dramatic flair?" Alex let out a choked cough from the driver's seat next to me that might have been covering a laugh.

Orion turned from where he was glaring out the window and stared at me with his heavy, black gaze. For a moment all my bravery fled, chilled by his dark scowl. Familiarity might breed contempt, but the contempt of a predator can get you killed. Finally he let out a long sigh, and his expression softened.

"The logo is from Homer," the Nephilim told us. I got the sense he was choosing his words with care. "It is a drawing of an island that Odysseus and his men sailed by on their return from Troy."

"Don't tell me you killed Odysseus," I said, holding up a hand. There were things I just didn't want to know. My mind raced, trying to think of all the islands the Greeks had sailed past on their way home. There had been a lot of them—that was most of Homer's *Odyssey*. None of them were great, from what I remember. *Please don't be a Cyclops,* I thought desperately.

"That island was home to one of the most dangerous creatures on the face of the earth," Orion continued, ignoring my interjection. "When I was younger, I killed her."

"Her?" I prompted.

"Peisinoe, the Siren."

The car was silent for a moment. I opened my mouth, then realized I had nothing to say and closed it again. There's a first time for everything, I guess.

"The Siren?" Alex managed after we had finally moved a dozen feet. "Like the music that drove men mad, and Odysseus had to be tied to the mast of his own ship?"

"Yes."

My friend and I exchanged a shocked glance. I guess it seems almost stupid to be surprised about a mythological creature being real given the life I lead. I've seen ghouls, Fae, a minotaur, and demons. Why shouldn't a Siren be real?

"What even was she?" I asked.

"A powerful shapeshifter." Sure, why not.

"I guess that explains how everyone died," I commented grimly, thinking about their beatific expressions. I had a fake college degree; it was a perk of Dan's meddling with my soul. But I had paid attention when we discussed the *Odyssey*. I'd even read it—well, most of it. I think I skipped a couple of the boring parts.

If memory served, the Siren's song had the ability to drive people mad and make them see a different reality. Sailors would inadvertently steer their ships onto the rocks. It seemed a trifling matter for that same ability to be used to make all three Nephilim hold their breath until they died or something. A shudder ran through me as I considered the implications of such power.

Orion grunted in agreement.

"But you killed her?" Alex prodded, trying to get Orion talking. "So it couldn't be her back again, right? It has to be some sort of coincidence."

"She's dead," the Hunter promised. I didn't doubt him. Killing was a thing he was pretty good at.

"Did you use the sword?" My eyes tracked across the car to where the blade rested in the other captain's chair, buckled in as if it were another passenger. The ruby in the hilt glinted in the fading afternoon light. That twinkle always made me feel like it was alive. Then again, the fact that I had a scar in the shape of its pommel burned into my palm gave me the impression it was aware of more than it should be.

"It was before I earned it," Orion replied after a moment. My ears perked up at that. I don't know a lot about his magic sword. I can think of a few instances of fiery swords in myth and legend, but they're just guesses. The big guy doesn't like to talk about it. All I know is that things that get stabbed by it die for real.

"How did you do it?" Alex's voice was just above a whisper. I shot him an amused glance, half surprised to see that he wasn't drooling. For all that my friend is two hundred years older than I am and a combat veteran, he's also just a huge Orion fan. I can't really blame him.

"I cut off her head and threw it into a volcano," Orion admitted after a moment. "Then I wrapped her corpse in chains and threw it into the sea."

That's what I'm talking about. He's just kind of a badass. I don't care what myth you compare him to, he stacks up. Achilles, Hercules, and Perseus could eat their freaking hearts out. Okay, maybe I'm a little bit of a fan too.

"That sounds pretty dead," I admitted. "Even if she was Immortal and not just—immortal?" The capitalization is important. Not all immortals are created equal. Lowercase individuals won't die of old age, but a bullet will kill them as easily as it would me. A being with a capital *I*, on the other hand, requires some extra killing. I'm beginning to suspect that there are also IMMORTALS, another rung up on the ladder, but I've never encountered one. Hopefully I never do.

"It worked for all the others," Orion replied with a shrug. So freaking cool.

Alex's eyes looked like they were about to pop out of his head. For once I was grateful for the 405's slow pace. My friend was so excited, I didn't trust him to be driving at top speeds for a little bit. I was pretty sure my seat didn't have an airbag.

"So if she's dead-dead," I continued, trying to follow along with the story, "Then from the card is from whom?"

"*Whom*?" Alex turns to look at me with incredulity.

"I was feeling English Major-y today."

"I don't know." Orion continued, ignoring our banter as he often did. "But they wanted whoever found the bodies to know who killed them."

"Why would someone leave a calling card?" I protested. "Isn't like the whole point of murder to get away with it?"

"Some people might get power out of claiming responsibility for their kills," Alex pointed out.

"Like whom?" Now that I had done it once, I couldn't stop myself. Sometimes technically correct is the best form of correct.

"Hit men? Professional killers?"

"Like, now they can put these murders on their résumé to raise prices on future kills?"

"It's a theory." Alex shrugged.

"It could also be for me," Orion growled.

"For you?" I blinked. "I know you killed the last one, but it seems a little extreme to assume it's all about you."

"LA is the Hunt's territory," Alex pointed out. "For someone to kill Nephilim here in this town and leave a calling card…"

"It's a challenge?" I asked, feeling incredulous. I turned back to the big man sitting in the seat behind me, hoping for an explanation. Orion was silent for a moment, which gave me time to think. When Dan stole my soul, Alex had gone to the Hunter for help. I had originally assumed that it was because he was a friend-of-a-friend. But since I had joined the Hunt, I'd realized it was so much more. Orion was the local big alpha. Not in the weird-wolf sort of sense, but more like an elder brother kind of way. If there was trouble with Nephilim, it had to go through him.

Because that was who Orion was. He watched out for the little guy, for the runts of his pack. I would know: I am one. Ever since Alex added me to the Hunter's list of people, he's watched out for me. In the Hunt, I've found a place I've been lacking all my life. A found family to replace the biological one I lost.

"If I cannot defend my territory, then I do not deserve to keep it," he replied at last, not turning from the window. "Someone thinks they can get away with hurting my people. They are wrong." Goosebumps prickled my arms as I heard the primal anger lurking in Orion's voice. Despite his rocky exterior, the big guy is something of a softie. Seeing the corpses of his cousins was eating at him like an acid.

"What are we going to do?" I could only assume it would be violent.

"First, we get answers."

"Then we kill them?" I used to be such a nice boy.

"Then we kill them."

AT ORION'S INSTRUCTION, we battled our way through LA rush hour to get to Hollywood, which turns into a war zone from 4 to 7 p.m. Alex and I both protested, but the Hunter insisted. Orion's a bit like a bloodhound; once he's got the scent, there's no stopping him. He's also bad at explanations. He didn't tell us where we were going or what we were doing—only that we needed to go this way.

Following his directions, we made our way down Hollywood Boulevard, where celebrities' names are stamped onto the sidewalk in stars like some pathetic imitation of the constellations above. Maybe that's where they got the idea.

We turned off the Walk of Fame and made our way through the ramshackle neighborhood that surrounds the country's most famous street. Having lived in Los Angeles my whole life, I've never understood tourists' obsession with this part of town. Once upon a time, it was supposed to have been something special, but those days are long past. Nowadays it's hot, dirty, and a little dangerous, depending on where you go.

You'll never find a celebrity here. They don't film movies in Hollywood anymore. The closest sets worth mentioning are in Burbank—a much more pleasant area. It's just nostalgia and marketing that keep the people rolling through. All that is to say, I don't make a habit of hanging out in this part of town, especially living on the other side of the 405 as I do. It's got nothing going for it.

After a few blocks, the Hunter told Alex to pull over. It took us ten minutes to find street parking that wasn't permit-only. Orion slung his blade over his shoulder as he slid out of the van. "Arm up," he grunted.

Alex and I traded knowing looks but didn't say anything. I popped open the glove compartment and pulled out a pair of nine-millimeter pistols, offering one to my friend. Four months ago ,I barely knew how to use one of these things. Since then, the Hunter has spent countless hours drilling both of us in armed combat, but it still felt surreal to this Californian to stuff a pistol down my pants as I got out of a van in broad daylight.

Armed and somewhat dangerous, Alex and I followed Orion as he stalked toward an apartment complex. It was an old five-story building, faded and brown. All of the windows had their curtains drawn shut like shields against the setting sun. A pair of glass doors led to a lobby, with an ancient callbox on one door.

Orion stalked up to the entrance and eyed the intercom for a moment. With a growl of irritation, he punched in a number combination, and the three of us lurked in awkward silence as the line began to ring in bursts of static.

"No." An old woman's voice came out of the intercom.

"Yes," Orion replied.

"I said no, Hunter."

"I'm not asking, hag," our boss snarled. His right hand curled into a fist, and I blinked in surprise to see him lose his cool.

"I will not invite you in," her voice hissed through the static-filled line, and suddenly I understood. Orion was part human, but he was also something more. The first time he came to my apartment, he'd insisted that I invite him in, just like you're not supposed to with vampires. Apparently if I hadn't, he'd have been forced to leave some of his supernaturalness at the door.

"Matthew, shoot out the glass." The Hunter's voice was coldly furious.

"Huh?" I snapped my head up from the intercom to share a nervous glance at Alex. My friend looked back at me with eyes as round as dinner plates. "You want me to what now?" I'd been in a couple of gunfights, but this was new. For the first time, it occurred to me that having two squires who were mostly mortal was a convenient loophole for Orion to get around the supernaturals-must-have-an-invitation rule. He could always send us in his stead.

"He won't do it," the voice chuckled in dry amusement.

"Shoot. Out. The. Door." Orion bit off each word. My heart was racing. I felt like I was being asked to murder something—maybe the peace, or the property values of this neighborhood. For some reason, pulling out my gun and blasting out an apartment building's front door on a Friday afternoon felt like a big ask.

"He's not going to do it," the woman repeated, exasperated. "Do you doubt what I know?"

"Matthew," Orion scolded without looking away from the callbox. It was like he was in a staring contest with the person on the other side. But there was no camera on it; I checked.

"Uh, are you sure?" I managed, slowly reaching for the weapon tucked in my waistband, just to seem like I was doing something. I wasn't sure I had the mettle to actually whip it out.

"I told you." Dark humor threaded itself into her voice. Orion ignored her and began to count, like a parent scolding a toddler.

"Three, two—" My hand tightened on the grip of the gun, and against my better judgment I began to draw it. I didn't really want to, but that's what being a squire is sometimes. When the big man says "shoot," I gotta pull the trigger.

"Enough," the voice sighed as if she felt me decide to obey. "I grow weary of this posturing. Come up, and let's get this over with." There was a loud buzz as she pressed the button to let us in. Orion yanked the door open as if afraid she would change her mind.

"What was that?" I demanded as I trotted in his wake. The Hunter ignored me, leading us to the elevator and pressing the UP button with enough force that I thought it might be stuck forever. Alex and I traded another set of nervous glances.

"Stop that," Orion snapped without turning, making both of us jump. It seems his hearing is so good, he can hear the sinews in our necks creak when we look around. Truly terrifying.

With a weak ding, the elevator doors opened, revealing a

small box with dirty linoleum and peeling wallpaper. The three of us managed to squeeze ourselves into the space, and Orion punched the button for FLOOR 4 with the same amount of aggression. The doors rumbled closed with an incredible lack of urgency.

Like everything else about the building, the elevator was old, and it shuddered as it began to lift us. I knew before the light for the second floor lit up that we should have taken the stairs. Alex and I shifted awkwardly in the tense silence. I would have done anything for some smooth jazz to play. Orion glared at the buttons as if he could threaten the ancient machine into going faster.

By the time we made it to the top floor, we were all fuming. I could have made the trip up the steps twice and still had time to catch my breath. When the doors ground open, we burst out, and once more I found myself trotting to keep up with the Hunter's long-legged strides.

The building had only five apartments on the floor, and Orion stopped at the center one, Unit 403. He drew his hand back to knock, but the door opened before his knuckles could land. There was no one there to greet us; the door simply swung open slowly as if blown by the wind. I shivered at the sight of the empty doorway. Where had Orion brought us?

"Come in, *Hunter*," called the woman's voice from within. "Let's get this over with. Oh, and don't step on the cat's dish, young man."

"Huh?" I asked just as my foot came down on an old china saucer, which shattered with a crack like a gunshot. I let out a little squeak and jumped to the side, but the damage was done. There was another sigh from the apartment's owner.

Satisfied with our invitation, Orion marched through the door. I was oddly reassured to see his right hand rise to hover near the hilt of his sword as he entered. At least I wasn't the only one getting a bad feeling about this. Following his lead, I reached for the grip of my pistol. Now that we were off the street and in someone's home, I didn't feel nearly as weird about drawing my gun.

"Oh, spare me the dramatics, Allslayer," the woman said, her voice wry with amusement. "If I wanted you dead, there would be much better ways to accomplish that than to invite you into my own home." At her words, Orion relaxed, his hand dropping to hover by his waist. I followed his lead; she had a point. Letting the Hunter into your home to kill him would be like the little pigs leaving their doors unlocked when the wolf was about.

I followed Orion down a short hallway covered with old wood panels from the 1960s. We passed an empty kitchen full of yellowing linoleum and peeling white countertops. At the end of the hall, we took a left and stepped into the living room, where an old black-and-white television was playing with the sound turned off. The place was heady with the smell of something burning—incense, unless I missed my guess.

A frail old woman sat in an overstuffed chair. She wore a matching sweatsuit set of faded gold. Her eyes were closed, sewn shut with a dark thread. A thrill ran through me like an electric shock as I took in her features. Somehow, I knew she saw me better than I saw her with my eyes open. Who was this woman that she chose not to see?

"It's been a long time, Hunter," she crooned, her eyelids trained on us in a stare that was somehow intimidating. "Here

I had begun to think you'd forgotten about me."

Orion did not reply for a moment, looming over the tiny woman like a skyscraper. They could not have been more physically different. If I were to guess, I'd say the big Nephilim weighed five or six times what the crone did. And yet there was a presence to her that rivaled the wired intensity radiating from my boss.

"I did not forget about you, Sibyl," he murmured. Before his tone had been cold and commanding, but now it was soft—or as soft as his voice could get, at any rate. "I chose to let you live in peace."

"Peace, ha!" The woman's laughter was as mocking as a crow's. "What peace can there be for one such as me, *Nephilim*?" Her tone made the word a curse. "Blind you may have made me, but still, I see far too well. There is no peace to be found for me."

Alex and I again traded glances behind Orion's back. The big man is intense. That's not news. But sewing this old crone's eyes shut? That showed a colder side to him than I had seen before. She looked like someone's grandmother, barely capable of hurting a fly.

Granted, if there's one thing I've learned in the last four months, it's that in the supernatural world appearances can be deceiving.

"You came to me for sanctuary," Orion replied after a long, pregnant moment.

"And the cost is more than I can bear," she snapped, turning her blind eyes away from us.

"You are alive."

"What life is this? I am a prisoner in the dark with only fading ghosts for company. You are the Hunter, not the King.

What right have you to demand such a thing of me?"

"You asked for my protection, and I gave you my price. If you wish to forfeit it, you are free to do so."

The woman gnashed her old, yellowing teeth in disgust. "Prison or death, a fine choice," she grumbled. "Enough of this. I am too old for this argument, and you are making me miss my shows. Why have you come?"

"What have you seen?" Orion asked after a moment.

"Nothing."

"Do not lie to me." A hint of Orion's usual iron tone crept back into his voice. To my surprise, Sibyl seemed to shrink in on herself on the chair, like a worm on a hot sidewalk.

"It doesn't work like that! I have *blind spots* now." She gestured at her sewn-shut eyes with dramatic flair. "Just because Beethoven could compose music after he went deaf doesn't mean I can still see."

Orion studied her. For the first time I realized that he was hesitating. He seemed like a man at the edge of a cliff, debating whether the water below was deep enough to catch him or if he would be dashed into pieces on the rocks.

He must have decided to risk it. Without a word he pulled out the calling card our killer had left behind and handed it to her. Sibyl took it and stared down at it with her closed eyes. A chill seemed to wash over her. The fiery resentment faded into the wind, replaced by the stiff spine of someone afraid to move.

"What have you seen?" Orion repeated softly.

"Nothing," she breathed in something like horror or awe. "I swear it."

"It cannot be a coincidence."

"You killed her," Sibyl protested. "I saw it with my own eyes."

"And since then? Nothing?"

"Nothing," she repeated fervently. "I would have told you." There was a note of genuine fear in the old woman's voice now. The fact that the calling card bothered her as much as it did Orion only served to heighten my sense of doom.

"She killed three of my people," he snarled at her, as if it were her fault.

"I am blind," she half whispered. Her voice shook with unreleased sobs. "I cannot see."

"Then perhaps it is time you did," the Hunter growled, his left hand darting forward to grab her face. The woman screamed and twisted in his grip, but she was caught fast like a bear in a trap. With a flick, Orion produced a pocketknife. I had to look away as he deftly sliced at her stitches.

"No," begged the woman, her earlier haughty complaints gone. "Please! Don't make me see."

"I helped you escape Delphi and have sheltered you for almost a century," Orion insisted. "I have never claimed the questions I am owed. Now I do." The woman let out another sob but did not protest further. The Hunter stepped back, apparently satisfied with his field surgery. I risked a look.

The old woman's eyelids fluttered open slowly. She was not bleeding; the Hunter was too dexterous to cut anything he did not wish to. But I recoiled in horror as her lids opened to reveal empty sockets beneath.

Sibyl stared at us with something like astonishment, as if she was no longer blind. Perhaps she wasn't, but whatever she saw was not with eyes. A power began to thrum in the room. I could feel it vibrating in my chest like I was standing too close to a transformer.

"*I see.*" Sibyl's hiss was somehow both triumphant and terrified. "*I am seen.*" A chill ran through me. What did those empty eyes peer into that could look bac? Nietzsche's famous line nagged at the back of my mind.

"The mark of the Siren has been used for the first time in centuries. What do you see?" Orion demanded, his knife still in hand. "Speak, Oracle. Tell me the three truths that I am owed." A wave of understanding swept over me. My knowledge of ancient myths was inconsistent, but even I had heard of the Oracle of Delphi. In retrospect, she looked great for her age.

"I see a flute," she proclaimed in haunted tones. "The daughter of the middle note plays a tortured song."

"Speak not in riddles," the Hunter commanded. "Tell me of the Siren."

"I see broken chains. I feel rushing water. I smell rot and death. But from the darkness comes light." Orion was silent, tall and brooding. If I was following the exchange, he only had one more question left. It was clear he wasn't satisfied with the answers he had been given so far. But I think that's sort of the deal with Oracles. They're prophets, not search engines.

"Tell me what this singer wants," he ordered at last, clearly unhappy with the question.

"I see a crown and a scepter with the whole globe resting on it. The world is bound in chains, there is nothing but the song. It is blinding! The Siren sings again! I cannot see, I cannot see!" The Oracle began to weep. For all her protests, it seemed she missed her vision once she lost it. Sibyl fell silent, her last shout echoing in her cheap apartment. I hovered behind Orion with bated breath. I didn't fully understand what was happening here. But it didn't seem like we were getting answers—only more questions.

Scary questions.

Sibyl let out a long sigh and deflated into her chair. She turned to regard Orion with a bitter expression. "A century you kept that bargain in your back pocket, and you waste it on this?"

"I did not waste it," he reprimanded her absently.

"I could have told you the weakness of Dra—"

"It was *not* wasted," he repeated, more forcefully. The Hunter is primal—there is no other word to describe him. His people had been killed, and he would do something about it. It wasn't a business decision or a selfish one. It was just who he was.

There are many ways to die horribly in this world, but murdering innocents who are protected by the Hunter and then taunting him must be pretty high up on the list. A shudder ran down my spine as I realized that I would have a front-row seat to the justice visited upon the perp.

"It didn't seem all that clear," Alex offered gently from my side. Orion twisted to stare at him as if he had forgotten we were here. Sibyl let out a dusty cackle.

"I can only proclaim what the Fates let me see, pup."

"But it's real?" I asked, still a little flabbergasted that I was in the presence of an Oracle. Yet another legend that I had thought was only a myth. Not for the first time, I wished I had paid more attention in school.

"What is real?" Sibyl demanded, turning to stare at me with her empty eyes. I opened my mouth to give her a glib reply, but I never got the chance. As her focus fell on me, her entire body locked up, like she'd been struck by lightning.

"What are you?" the woman who could see the tapestry of Fate demanded. That question was more terrifying to me than almost anything else she could have said. Thanks to Dan the demon, my life was on an unusual path, but when an Oracle is stumped, that seems like a bad sign.

"I'm Matt," I told her.

"You are cattle," she replied scornfully as she continued studying me. "Bought and sold like livestock." Despite my innocence on that whole thing, an embarrassed flush crept up my neck. It's sort of mortifying when supernatural beings can tell that you've sold your soul to the Devil. It's like reeking of alcohol before noon.

"I am not cattle," I insisted hotly, taking a step toward the seated Oracle.

"I see nothing but the path of Death for you."

"Everyone dies," I scoffed. "What kind of fortune is that?"

"For you, there is no fortune." Despite my irritation at this old woman's judgment, a chill settled on me, wrapping around me like a wet blanket. No matter how hard I tried to shake it off, it only stuck to me further.

"Enough," Orion growled, interrupting our exchange.

"I know, Hunter," Sibyl grumbled bitterly. "It is time." Turning, she reached over to a small table next to her chair and pulled out a needle and a spool of black thread. I could only stare in horror as she began to thread it, preparing to sew her eyes shut once more.

"I've paid your price, now get out of my house."

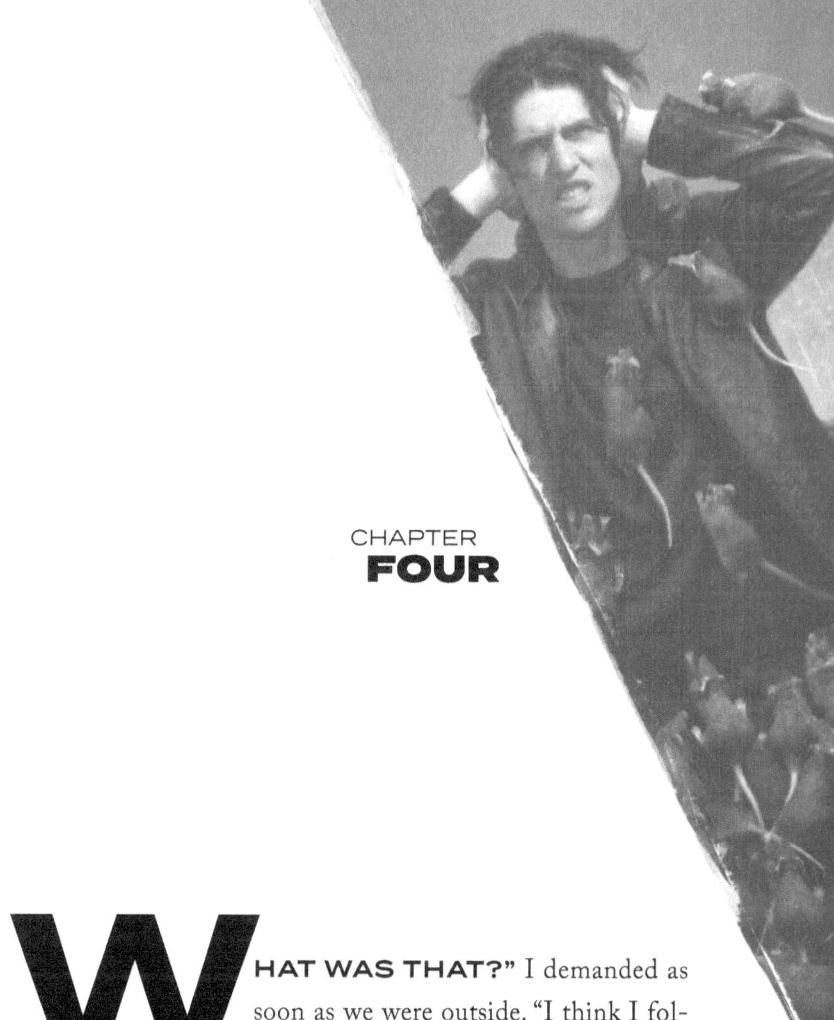

WHAT WAS THAT?"** I demanded as soon as we were outside. "I think I followed most of it, but was that really the Oracle of Delphi?"

"She was once," Orion corrected, not breaking his stride as we trooped back to Alex's van. "Now another holds that position."

"So she's just *an* Oracle? There's more than one?"

"I think there are supposed to be five," Alex offered from beside me.

"There are always five. One is in Delphi; the other sites are not as well known. Cumae, Didyma, Dodona, and Abae must each have an Oracle in residence."

"Is it a position, like being a senator?" I interjected. Cumae sounded familiar to me, but the rest might as well have been French, although I suspected they were Greek.

"There are more people born with the sight of an Oracle than there are seats for them," Orion continued, ignoring my question. "When a new one is found, they kill the old one." So that's what she had meant about Orion helping her escape and sheltering her. She was literally on the run. I shouldn't have been surprised to find out that the big Nephilim had other strays he had taken care of. I wasn't his first project, just the newest one.

"She's a sixth Oracle?" Alex added, clearly following the same thought process as me.

"When she saw that her replacement had been born, she asked for my help to escape from Delphi. As we sailed away from Greece, the Siren sought to stop us. I disabused her of that notion."

"What's the deal with her eyes and the thread?" I skipped to the good part. It was too creepy not to ask about.

"She plucked out her eyes and sewed them shut to help her hide. It makes it harder for her to see Fate." That sounded horrible, but I couldn't help but feel a small amount of respect for anyone willing to go to those lengths to survive. I would do anything to get my soul back. Well—just about anything. Cutting out my own eyes felt like it was getting close to the line.

"How does that help her hide? Seems like seeing Fate would be a handy way to stay ahead of anyone chasing you."

"It makes the other Oracles struggle to see her. It's not about what she sees when she looks through Fate," Orion replied grimly, "but about what looks out her eyes while she does."

A shudder ran through me. "*I am seen,*" she had said. "So you have her hidden under a bushel, or whatever, but you made her expose herself to investigate the murders?"

"That was the price she offered for my help. Her debt is now paid."

"Well, I hope you don't have buyer's remorse, because that did not seem to be the most useful information," I pointed out.

"It told me what I needed to know."

"Which was?" Alex prompted, something of an exasperated tone in his voice.

"The Siren Peisinoe is still dead." Grim satisfaction flooded through the Hunter's voice. "Which means that whoever left the mark of the Siren at the scene of the crime is merely a pretender." But I thought I understood what he had been worried about. The killer had used the calling card of an old enemy of the Hunter, and it had been worth using his questions to confirm her death.

"Didn't she say that the Siren's song was being played again? There was a lot of talk about music," I pointed out. "That sounds like a Siren to me."

"Any other song is some pretender, claiming to be something that is gone," the Hunter asserted. I guess that meant that whoever was pretending to be a Siren wouldn't be as powerful as Peisinoe had been. The copy is never as good as the original.

"What do you make of all that stuff about rushing water and breaking chains? That sounded pretty bad," Alex pointed out.

"Something about light too," I remembered.

Orion contemplated his response. "It means someone is digging into things that should be forgotten—stirring up old trouble."

"There was also something about the daughter of the middle

note?" I asked, glancing at Alex for help. "Any idea who that is?"

"I'm guessing that is Mese, who is sometimes called Apollonis," Alex suggested, glancing at Orion through the rearview mirror. "She was the middle Muse of Delphi."

"And the Muses are different from the Oracles how?"

"Different departments," Alex told me. "Fates dictate. Oracles prophesy. Muses inspire."

"Obviously," I replied, regretting that I asked. "So, something to do with one of her daughters?"

"That's what it sounded like to me," Alex agreed. "Any idea who that might be?"

"No, but Driscoll can investigate. Get him on it," Orion replied. I nodded and pulled out my phone. Constellations don't make their own calls. That's what squires are for.

"What do we do next?" I asked as the line began to ring. This felt like something bigger than I was equipped to handle. I was no cop; how was I supposed to help solve murders?

"We start rattling the trees and see who falls out of the branches."

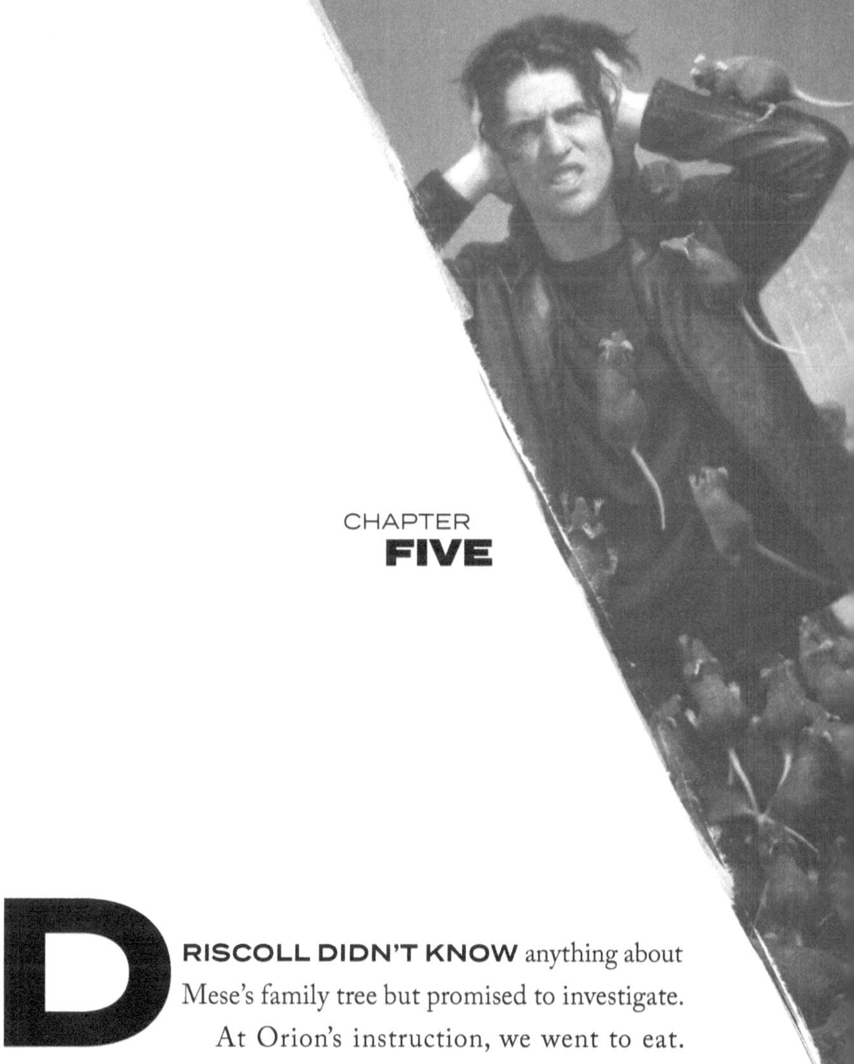

DRISCOLL DIDN'T KNOW anything about Mese's family tree but promised to investigate. At Orion's instruction, we went to eat. Which was fine with me, because detectiving is a hungry job. No wonder there's a stereotype about law enforcement and doughnuts.

The supernatural community exists in uneasy tandem with its mortal cousins. Many Nephilim, Fae, and other beings can walk down the street without anyone ever noticing. But like any other mortal, they appreciate spaces where they can be themselves.

There are places that are designed to attract only the initiated. I've never really figured out how they do it. My guess is some sort of magic in the paint repelling normals. The Mount Olympus Bar and Grille is one such place. Before Dan stole my soul, I had walked past it a thousand times without ever giving it a second glance. But the day after, it leapt out to me like a beacon. For any regular human eating there, I imagine the experience would be like finding yourself in a restaurant that seems popular but feels like everyone is holding their breath, waiting for you to leave. I wonder how many other places like that I went to before I knew what to look for.

The Grille is a squat little structure set between two taller buildings, like a café sandwich. It has swinging doors that always make me think of a Wild West saloon, and its food is surprisingly bad for how popular it is. A cluster of dandelions grew in a planter hanging from the front porch, which gave me pause. Ever since Robin the Faerie had told me that his Queen wanted to speak with me, I had been seeing a lot more of the little fluffers around. They were apparently her preferred method of communication, but I was starting to feel like they were following me. Honestly, it wouldn't be the weirdest thing I had learned in the last four months.

The Hunter led us up the steps to those iconic doors and burst through them with the melodramatic flair that only a man who has a constellation wrought in his image can summon. The diner went silent. The place was engulfed in a complete and total stillness, like the woods after someone fires a gun.

The inside of the Grille looks like a classic 1950s-style diner. A long bar ran along the right side of the room, with a mirror and hundreds of bottles behind it. On the left was a row of plasticky booths; a mishmash of scattered tables and chairs filled the middle.

It being just after dusk on a Friday, the room was beginning to fill up, and supernatural beings of every flavor turned to stare at the disrupting Hunter. He had their undivided attention, but none dared to question him. The place was like a watering hole on the savanna, and the various denizens that hung out were like water buffalo, elks, and gazelles. They each had a pecking order and carved out their own space around the room. But now a lion had come and upset the peace. Many of them were getting ready to run.

Orion stuffed a hand into his black leather jacket and pulled out the Siren's card. He held it up for the room to see. If this had been a mortal bar, the gesture would have been wasted: Human eyes aren't good enough to see detail at that range. But even a drop of demon blood seems to give its host incredible vision. It's just not fair. Why did my parents have to be so *normal*? I could have been so much better at sports!

"If any of you know this mark, tell me." The room shifted uncomfortably, and I saw more than a few people look away from the Hunter. Whether that was because they had information or simply because they were caught up in a tense moment, I could only guess. No one offered any response. "If I discover that any of you do know what this is and are remaining silent, you will answer to me." The threat in his voice was colder than the industrial freezers in the kitchen.

Somehow holding eye contact with an entire room, Orion tucked the card back in his jacket and stomped forward, nodding with his head for us to fall in line. Like loyal ducklings, we squires followed in his wake. As usual, I felt the pressure of the room's attention as their gazes slowly slipped from the boss to his two surprising associates.

By supernatural bloodline standards, Alex and I should not have been playing in the big leagues. The original Hunt, as I understand it, was staffed with some heavy hitters until they met an untimely end that Orion definitely doesn't like talking about. Seeing us on the starting roster—well, it's as if the Lakers lost their star players and started recruiting high schoolers.

I agreed with the patrons, but it was still rude of them to stare so loudly.

We dropped into our usual booth at the end of the row, a large semicircular affair that always leaves me trapped in the middle. I hate it, but I don't get a vote. When Orion sat down, the room's conversation jerked back to life as if someone had plugged the jukebox back in.

"You know, I don't know if that was the best play," I remarked to the brooding Nephilim sitting at my left. "Do you guys have the saying *Snitches get stitches*, or is that only a mortal thing?"

"We usually say *Suturas ut suturis*, but I think it's the same idea," Alex offered.

"You know I hate it when you speak Latin to me." The last time I read anything in Latin, I accidentally summoned a demon, and it was the *wrong* demon. I could stand never to hear the language again.

"Someone will come forward," Orion interjected, ignoring our banter. Surprised, I glanced at the big guy. He did not possess what I would call an overactive sense of humor, but even the Hunter can appreciate a good joke from time to time.

He was different today.

To be fair, we had been at a murder scene only a few hours

ago. Maybe if my whole personality wasn't built around using humor as a shield to keep me from having to think thoughts that are itchy, I would know there were times that weren't appropriate for a joke.

He had to be under a tremendous weight of responsibility, I realized. How could he not feel like this was his fault? Not only was this his territory and his people, but the killer had clearly wanted to get his attention. I still thought that was a stupid idea. I have seen Orion's attention focused on an enemy; it does not seem a good time.

"What'll it be, boys?" Alice asked as she swept by our tables. The young Nephilim had served us a dozen times before. "Can I grab you something to drink?" The staff were more used to Orion's moody visits than the guests. Maybe it was because they knew he was never looking for them when he came.

"We won't be here long," Orion promised, stopping me from ordering a milkshake.

"Sure. If you change your mind let me know." She bounced away, unbothered by the Constellation.

"How do you know?" I complained. I hadn't felt like eating after the crime scene, but my appetite had finally come back. "We might have time for a snack."

"No," Orion insisted, his black eyes sweeping the room like a watchdog. "Someone will break very soon." Confused, I scanned the diner too, trying to see what he was looking at. But all I saw were slightly nervous patrons going about their normal Friday-afternoon happy hour.

"How can you tell?" Alex asked the question for both of us.

"I can hear their hearts." The Hunter tapped his right ear with one long finger. "Someone is panicking."

"Could it be because you're very, very scary?" I suggested.

"That is exactly it. Excuse me." Across the room, a man had stood from a table with his friends and was making his way toward the back of the diner. He strolled at a nonchalant pace with his hands in his pockets. He looked like he was heading to the bathrooms in the back.

Orion was on his feet as the man vanished down the back hall, drifting behind him with the languid grace of a panther stalking its prey. Alex and I exchanged nervous glances as our boss left us behind.

"I hate when he does this," my friend sighed before scrambling out of the booth. I crawled out of my cramped middle seat, and together we rushed toward the rear hall. I could feel the eyes of the room on the back of my neck as we went. Subtlety is not really part of the Hunt's repertoire.

Alex and I rounded the corner to the restrooms in time to see Orion's legs disappear through the door to the alley. "Here we go again," my friend grumbled. I held out my fist, and he rapped his knuckles against mine. As one, we broke into a sprint and burst out the back, following our master.

Orion was already half a block away from us, his legs pumping as he chased the fleeing man who was now running at full speed, like a gazelle. Alex and I thundered on their heels, but we didn't gain on the Hunter. The first thing Orion had begun training us on when we became his squires was cardio. There is an obnoxious amount of running involved in the work of the Hunt. I can run three miles without stopping, but there is no catching a cheetah when it is going for the kill.

Like a speeding arrow, Orion closed the distance between him and his target. He reached out with a long arm, grabbed the man's shoulder, and shoved him into the wall of the alley. The smaller man bounced off it like a tennis ball and fell to the ground.

Orion was looming over him when Alex and I caught up. The Hunter hadn't even broken a sweat. He glared down at the man with the patience of an eagle waiting to swoop. Our quarry lay there in a defeated puddle. He was conscious but seemed too depressed to move.

"Get up," the Hunter commanded after a long moment. The man stirred and sat up, leaning back against the wall with a defeated slump in his shoulders. Now that I was close, I could see the telltale features of a Nephilim lurking in his visage. His scraggly black hair hung past his ears, but I could just make out the pointed tips through the jungle. His jaw was a little too sharp. But his eyes were mortal. A lesser Nephilim then, more like Alex than Orion.

"I'm a dead man," he sighed, closing his eyes.

"I'm not here to kill you," Orion rumbled in reply.

"You think you're what I'm scared of, Hunter?" A laugh of disbelief bubbled from his chest. "You're a man of honor. Everyone knows that. It's not you I'm worried about."

"Who?" The darkness in his voice was like a storm gathering on the horizon. It gave me chills, and I wasn't even its intended target.

"People with more power even than you."

To my surprise, Orion dropped into a crouch, making his gaze level with that of the downcast man. For a moment he looked at the runner, and something close to pity began to bloom on his face. "What is your name?" he asked abruptly.

"David."

"Well, David, it seems that you have a decision to make," Orion said softly. Gone was his anger, replaced by something steady, like the foundations of the earth. The Hunter pulled the calling card out of his pocket and held it up. "This Siren's Seal was left with the bodies of three Nephilim."

David let out a choked moan of despair.

"You're right: The person responsible for these deaths will kill you. I will not kill you, but if you help me, I may be able to stop them from killing you."

"You don't know what you're up against."

"I have an idea," Orion replied drolly. "I killed the Siren in the first place. This pretender is but a shadow of the true monster." David's head came up at that, and his mouth opened slightly in shock. I guess he hadn't known that either.

"You really are what they say you are, aren't you?"

In response, Orion merely tilted his head back and looked up into the sky. LA's light pollution makes stargazing something of a rare activity, but in the twilight, the three bright stars in a line that make up his belt burned above us. David followed his gaze, and before my eyes I saw some of his stress bleed away. Orion's credentials are hard to argue with.

"Besides," I offered into the stillness of that moment, "if they know you spoke with Orion, they're going to assume you snitched anyway." David closed his eyes and took a deep breath, like a man preparing to plunge into icy water.

"I don't know who she is," he told us without opening his eyes. "But I saw a woman with that tattoo take out an entire security team of our kind."

"Go on," Orion urged.

"I work at a warehouse that handles shipping for items

mortals shouldn't see. Antiques, artifacts, things like that. Three nights ago, this chick walks right into our facility and starts cutting into a shipping container with a blowtorch. No subtlety or anything, just right out in the open.

"We scramble our response team, a bunch of Nephs that aren't as intimidating as you, sir, but they're still some tough operators. Or were, I guess. They surrounded her, went in with weapons hot, and she killed them all."

"How?" I had a really bad feeling that I knew exactly how they had died.

"She pulled out some sort of flute and started playing it, and the world fell apart. I was up in the control room, but even I felt it. Reality changed, and all of a sudden I saw monsters where the guards had been. I guess they saw the same thing and shot one another." I exchanged concerned glances with the other members of the Hunt. That sure sounded like a Siren to me.

"I'm pretty sure I only survived because there was no one in the room with me to shoot me." The man's Adam's apple bobbed in his throat as he swallowed. I couldn't blame him.

"What are you worried about?" Alex chuckled. "Sounds like she has no idea you exist."

David shook his head. "After that, a couple of guys came in to help her carry out the stuff from the crate. They were all robotic, like drones. While they took everything, she saw the camera." He shuddered. "She played me a song that told me what would happen to me if I spoke to anyone."

"A bluff," Orion scoffed.

"What did they take?" I asked.

"I don't know—we don't have access to the manifests. We

just make sure the crates get on the right trucks and no one takes them."

"Maybe that career isn't for you," I pointed out, earning a glare from the seated Nephilim. I guess this wasn't the time.

"Where is this warehouse?" Orion demanded.

"Not far," David replied, giving him the address.

"Let's go," the Hunter said, turning to us. It was going to be a long night. I really wished I'd had time to order something.

"What about me, you gotta protect me!" David begged, a plaintive note entering his voice.

"I will," Orion promised, turning to me. "Call—" The guard let out a gasp, interrupting Orion. The three of us spun back to David, eyes wide. The Nephilim fell to his knees, hands clawing at his throat.

"Breathe, man!" Alex shouted, pounding him on the back. David fell to all fours, hacking in the alley like a dog.

"Hunter," he wheezed, his voice warped and twisted. "I hoped it would be you. Watch as another one of your precious celestial cousins dies." The thing spoke with David's voice, but it did not sound like his words. It was as if something had been left in his brain, waiting for Orion.

Quick as a snake, Orion's fist slammed into the back of David's head, right at the base of his skull. The smaller Nephilim collapsed bonelessly to the ground, a sack of meat.

"Dude, what the hell—" I shouted, turning to our boss in shock, but he interrupted me by holding up a single finger. Together the three of us watched as David's body relaxed, and his breathing became normal. Despite being unconscious, he seemed fine.

Orion let out a satisfied grunt after a moment and turned

back to me. "The Siren's song cannot control your subconscious. It can't strangle him if he's not awake to strangle himself."

"Did you know that was going to work?" Alex demanded.

"It was a good guess." The two of us stared at Orion in stunned silence. Then he yanked us back into action. "Matt, have Driscoll watch over him. Tell him to keep David sedated until we tell him otherwise." I pulled out my phone to make another call.

"When will that be?"

"Once the one who played the song is dead."

CHAPTER
SIX

HAVE BAD LUCK with a lot of things, but warehouses are high up on the list. I've already burned one down this year. Well, technically *I* didn't burn that one down, but it was sort of my fault that it got crisped. Based on that track record, I didn't have the greatest feeling as we pulled up to this one.

The warehouse was one of many in the area surrounding the Port of Los Angeles. Row upon row of squat, uninteresting buildings sat like giant toads, holding imports and exports. We parked Alex's van in the almost empty front parking lot. Orion was already out the door before the car had finished moving.

I hopped out and followed him, ignoring the dandelion growing by the parking berm. Had that been there when we pulled up, or had it grown in the time it took us to park? Some people are haunted by ghosts; my specters have chlorophyll. Maybe they're not as scary as some undead monster, but they were starting to creep me out.

My bad feeling was immediately magnified when I noticed the sign on the door. Stamped in the center was a familiar logo, a sheaf of wheat surrounded by a sickle and stars. It was the logo of a mortal who dabbled in the supernatural business.

Lazarus.

The three of us drew up short as we stared at that seal. David hadn't mentioned who owned the warehouse, and it certainly added a layer of complexity to the situation. We currently had something of an uneasy truce with the businessman. I had more than enough enemies and wasn't eager to add any more to the list.

After a long moment, Orion drew back his fist and knocked on the door. Which indicated how seriously he took the owner-ship status of this place. A loud silence echoed through the night.

Orion paused, then knocked a second time, followed by a third. I could feel a tension brewing in him, like pressure in a volcano, and I prayed for all our sakes that someone would answer the freaking door before he erupted. He's a patient man, but only up to a point.

Showing an incredible amount of restraint, the Hunter went for a fourth knock, but before his fist could connect, the door swung open. Three men in tactical gear stood on the other side with assault rifles pointed at us in a business-like manner.

My heart skipped a beat as I stared down those barrels. I carry a gun, but that does nothing to make them any less in-timidating when they're pointed at you. If anything, it makes them even more terrifying. Every fiber of my being told me to raise my hands, but Orion didn't so much as twitch, so I did my duty and followed suit.

"Go home, Hunter," the man in the middle said, his voice cold and professional. "This is private property."

"Tell your master that I am here. He knows why." The three guards did not move for a moment, but I got the sense that someone had heard the order and was making a call. We stood in rigid silence. A couple of the guards warily eyed the sword peeking over Orion's shoulder. Given what it could do, I didn't blame them at all.

The quiet lasted long enough for my brain to begin to work against itself. What would we do if Lazarus refused to admit us? That part was sort of a rhetorical question. There would be no stopping Orion from going in. But if we had to carve our way past three armed guards, I really didn't like my odds of not being shot.

The pistol I had been carrying in my back waistband all day felt heavy. As I stood there, tensed to spring into action, it was all I could think about. Mentally I rehearsed ducking into a crouch and grabbing the pistol in one fluid motion.

I would go for the guy on the right. He was wearing body armor, so it was unlikely that my nine-millimeter rounds would do more than knock him down, but that would buy Orion enough time to close with his sword. Once these guards were down, I could take one of their rifles and use that—

The middle guard's radio squawked. He tilted his head, listening to the feed in his ear, then nodded once. Slowly, he lowered his weapon, and his squad mates followed suit. "Boss says you can come in."

We followed the security team into the bowels of the dimly

lit art warehouse. They gave us the professional courtesy of not asking us why we were there. Instead they led us right to the scene of the crime, so to speak. As we marched through the yawning expanse, I couldn't help but gape at the sheer number of crates that sat in here.

It felt a little like walking through the backroom of a museum. Most of the items were sealed up, but some were in the process of being packaged or simply so recognizable that it didn't matter. I saw a worn marble column that had to be from some ancient Greek temple. There was a whole row of what could only be paintings sealed in plywood boxes. I'd be only a little surprised to discover that some of the missing works of Old Masters were boxed up in this place.

When David explained what this place was for, I should have realized that this was exactly the kind of thing Lazarus did. He was a semi-philanthropic billionaire who was obsessed with the world beyond ours. He owned an entire medical arm dedicated to finding a cure for death. Of course he would be interested in supernatural artifacts too.

The center of the warehouse housed even more collections. The guards walked us down a row of metallic shipping crates, and we stopped at one that had been cut open. Just as David had described, the bolts of the lock had been sliced, and the door hung ajar. The bodies were long gone, but even in the low light I could see the red stains on the ground where the guards had shot one another. Knowing how they died made the scene even more eerie to look at.

The three guards stepped to the side and watched us with flat expressions. Orion ignored them and began to pace around the outer edge of the scene, black eyes narrowed. Alex and I followed in his wake like obedient shadows.

Something felt off to me about all this. David said the robbery and killings had happened three days ago. The murder victims we had seen earlier today had been dead for a day and a half, which meant they were killed soon after this robbery.

But what connected them? Orion had taken the killing of Nephilim in his territory as a personal challenge, but as far as I knew, someone choosing to rob Lazarus was an entirely different thing—even if his employees were Nephilim.

"What was in the crate?" I asked the guards, still trailing after Orion, trying to look where he did. They ignored me, and I rolled my eyes. "Your boss told you to let us in," I reminded them. "There's no point in being all evasive now."

"They don't know," came a voice from the darkness. Startled, I turned in time to see the man himself emerge from the gloom, walking with his golden cane. It clicked on the cement floor with each step as he drew nearer.

Lazarus looked like a run-of-the-mill tenured literary professor. I've never seen him not in a tweed suit, and his gray hair went perfectly with his horn-rimmed glasses. Steel lurked beneath the surface of the old man—a vitality that had not even begun to fade from him. He too was dangerous, but in a different way.

Orion paused his pacing to watch the approaching businessman with dark eyes. The last time we had a meeting with Lazarus, he had been respectful. But there was plenty of tension between the Hunter and the gangster. They looked like two dogs staring at each other through a fence.

"But you do?" I challenged.

"Of course, Mr. Carver." Lazarus's glasses flashed as he gave me an almost reproachful look. There was an implied threat in his manner that I did not like. It said: *You know what happens if you cross me, boy*. But he was right, I did.

"Care to share with the class?" Alex asked, interposing himself into our little staring contest.

"Because he looks like a teacher?" I arched an eyebrow at my friend.

"It was right there." Alex shrugged as if he couldn't be held liable—and in his defense, what was he supposed to do, ignore it?

If Lazarus heard our fashion critique, he ignored it, dismissing us as unruly students and training his gaze back on the Hunter. "It was the remains of a creature that defied identification. We purchased the body from a group of explorers who found it at the bottom of the sea." A chill ran through me. I knew where this was going. The Oracle had spoken of broken chains and rushing water. That must have been the explorers discovering Peisinoe's remains down in the dark.

"Which sea?" Orion asked in a dangerous voice.

"The Aegean." The mobster's expression hardened as he saw the reaction to his words run across our faces. "I see you know this story," he murmured. I turned to see what Orion would say. The big Nephilim was still, a frown fixed firmly on his face.

"What condition were these remains in?" he demanded after a few moments.

"That is not how this is going to work, Hunter," Lazarus replied mildly. "Already I have invited you into my domain and given you information for free. I am no Faerie, but if you wish to learn any more, you must deal with me fairly."

Orion paused, then nodded once. "Question for question," he offered.

"What was it?" A hunger gleamed in Lazarus's eyes. For all that I made fun of him for looking like an academic, he played the part well. This was a man who thirsted for arcane knowledge and would do anything to get it.

"Peisinoe."

"Homer's Siren? Fascinating," he murmured. "You're certain?"

"That is your second question," Orion pointed out.

Lazarus waved the concern away, "I keep my deals, Hunter."

"I slew her myself."

"You truly are everything they say, aren't you?" A knowing glint ran through Lazarus's eyes. "That one is rhetorical, of course, since we're keeping score."

"What condition were these remains in?" Orion repeated. The big guy was wound tight. He's not a big emoter, but this was clearly pushing his buttons. He might hold a mixture of human and demon DNA, but if someone discovered that one of his great-grandfathers had been a rock, I wouldn't be that shocked. Now that I had spent so much time with him, however, I knew what to look for. The crease in the corner of his eyes was a telltale sign that he was worried. And when Orion worries, *I* start worrying. Was he afraid of some sort of resurrection? Was that possible for a creature like a Siren despite what the Oracle had said?

"Bones and some desiccated flesh." Lazarus shrugged as if not particularly bothered. "We had been unable to categorize it, but there wasn't much left to work with."

"What do you know of the people who stole her from you?" All of us gave him a surprised look at his use of a pronoun. I mean I knew it was *technically* correct, but it sure made her seem a lot more alive than if he'd referred to *the body*. Once again, I was struck by how weird my problems had become since I'd been thrown into the Hunt. Even if I got my soul back, how could I ever go back to my old, boring life?

I probably couldn't. But that was future Matt's problem. As present Matt, I only had to worry about not dying thanks to the musical killers that were after the Hunter's friends. Which technically included me. How had I just now realized that?

"Less than I'd like," Lazarus admitted gruffly. When knowledge is your arena, having to say that you don't know something has to sting. "The woman is an operator who calls herself the Pied Piper, for what I assume are obvious reasons. There have been no demands, and none of my connections have heard of the remains being sold to the usual actors. I have no idea who might have hired her."

"As in the fairy tale?" I asked in shocked surprise. I guess Alex was right about the whole calling-card thing. She left the card because she did want credit. The Pied Piper being an assassin was not on my bingo card.

"I said 'obvious reasons' on purpose, Mr. Carver," Lazarus replied with a sneer.

"Didn't the original one, like, get hired to lead a bunch of rats out of the city, then not get paid, so he bewitched all their children?" I ignored his scorn. I'd been ignoring teachers' opinions of me most my life; it wasn't that hard.

"Is there a point you're trying to make?"

"That sure sounds like a Siren to me. Wasn't Peisinoe busy luring boats to crash into her island?"

"That is actually relevant," Lazarus allowed, blinking in surprise. I tried not to find that too offensive.

"Say, what do you think she did with the kids she took?" I glanced between the two old guys. "Did they ever get found?"

"I suspect they're long dead."

Orion grunted, uninterested in our theories. He turned back to the scene, resuming his inspection.

The old man's eyes narrowed. "I told you what I know. What do you know of them?"

Absently, Orion dug the calling card out of his jacket pocket and tossed it toward me. He'd had his fill of talking, I guess. The big guy is more of a *doer* at the end of the day. I managed to snag the little black piece of card stock out of the air on my third try and turned to face Lazarus with what little dignity I had left. As the old man's attention settled on me once more, I felt my heart rate pick up. The gangster had too many pieces of my world in his hands for me to feel comfortable around him.

"A little birdy told us that the woman who led the attack had a tattoo that matched this on her face. Can you verify that?" I held up the card so that he could see the logo. The corner of his eye twitched in surprise, which was more than enough confirmation for me. "This is the logo—"

"Seal," Orion interjected without turning around.

"—the seal of the Siren." I pointed at the little rock in the center. "She lived on this very island until her untimely demise."

"Where did you get this?" Lazarus asked, eyes narrowing once more. I hesitated, not sure if this was my secret to tell. I glanced over my shoulder at Orion, who nodded once without turning around. Seriously, how did he know?

"We found it with the bodies of three murdered Nephilim earlier today."

"My condolences," Lazarus said, glancing at the Hunter

with something like genuine sincerity in his voice. I guess he understood the implications of that even better than I did. "You fear retribution?"

"I fear nothing," Orion growled without turning. "But I suspect these are connected, yes."

"Obviously," Lazarus replied caustically. He paused for a moment, considering something. "It seems to me, gentlemen, that in this matter we are both members of the aggrieved party. I propose an alliance."

My jaw dropped as I stared at the old academic. It made an odd sort of sense; I just couldn't believe that it had come out of his mouth. While we weren't enemies, there was enough murkiness between our two groups to keep us from ever eating lunch at the same table in the cafeteria of life. The Hunter didn't really play well with others, so I was certain that he'd tell the mobster where he could shove—

"Agreed," Orion answered. My head whipped around so fast, I thought I heard my sinews creak. I caught a glimpse of Alex across from me, staring at our boss with a similar shocked expression. I think I had been dramatically underestimating the severity of this situation. Which was monumentally stupid when I had seen him burn a centuries-old favor with a forgotten Oracle for a clue.

Like I said, when Orion starts to worry, *I worry.*

"Terms?" Lazarus asked.

"Complete sharing of information in regard to the name and location of the group that perpetrated this attack against you and my kin."

"Very well. You get your vengeance, Hunter. In exchange, I want my property back." Lazarus waited until Orion nodded in agreement. Then he smiled smugly, pulled a business card out of his pocket, and passed it to me. I glanced down to see that it was blank except for a phone number. "How can the Lazarus corporation be of assistance to the Hunt?"

"Do you have a picture of the woman's face?" I gestured at the ceiling. "I'm sure there's a dozen security cameras pointed at us right now."

"Of course." Lazarus snapped his fingers, and one of his hovering guards trotted off into the gloom, presumably to fetch our information.

"Was she injured?" Alex asked, jerking his thumb at the scene behind us. "Did she leave behind any blood or hair?"

"I am afraid she was quite professional," Lazarus replied with a shake of his head. "But now that you have given me more context about the nature of the remains that were stolen, perhaps my team will be able to produce more results from our contacts. We shall begin our inquiries immediately." Something about the way he said "inquiries" made me shiver.

The missing guard returned with a folder, which he passed to me at his boss's direction. I flipped it open and rifled through a series of printed security stills. They showed a woman with golden hair and sharp cheekbones. She wore a black tactical vest with matching combat fatigues. Around her right eye the line drawing of the seal of the Siren was inked onto her face, so that her eye was in the center of the island.

The next couple of pictures showed her producing a white flute and bringing it to her mouth. After that, masked men carried things out of the shipping container while she watched, the dark forms of dead security guards lying at her feet. Creepy.

"Well, I've certainly never seen her before," I commented

dryly, passing the brief to Alex. "I'd remember that particular tattoo."

"It will make it hard for her to hide from me," Lazarus agreed darkly.

"Do you have a recording of the song she played?" I was dreading the answer. I didn't want to hear something that had made a group of men kill their friends. I've seen a few horrors since I got this job, but this seemed like one I was happy to skip.

To my relief Lazarus shook his head. "Whatever music that pipe produces defied being captured by recording devices, I am afraid."

"That is probably for the best," Orion mused, clearly tracking with my thoughts.

"Is there anything else?" Lazarus asked mildly.

"We're done here," Orion replied, rising from his crouch and beginning to stride away. "We'll be in touch."

CHAPTER
SEVEN

MY PHONE RANG as we pulled out of Lazarus's parking lot. The sun was long gone over the horizon, and the industrial district was a sharp contrast of dark night and harsh streetlights. I glanced at my phone and saw it was Driscoll. "Hunt's office, this is Matt speaking," I said as I answered the phone.

"Matt, it's Driscoll," the Nephilim lawyer told me unhelpfully. I know he's probably super old, but we've had caller ID for a couple of decades. "I've got a lead on the Muse's offspring. A name and address."

"Mese's kid?" I asked, digging for a napkin and pen from Alex's center console. The other two members of the Hunt perked up at my tone.

"More like great-great-grandchild, but as close as I can find."

"Hit me," I said, clicking the pen.

"Her name is Harmony Cliff; she lives in Pasadena, off Backus Avenue."

"We'll check it out. Thanks, Driscoll."

"Good hunting."

I hung up and glanced around the car. It was well past 9 p.m., which for any normal job would mean we were off the clock and heading home. But that wasn't how this worked. People's lives were on the line, and rest was a luxury we could not afford. The Oracle had made it sound like the Muse's daughter would be in trouble. Well, that was my interpretation, but I felt safe in making the assumption. The plus side was that by doing our hero work at night, we got around town like ten times faster. When there's no traffic, LA is practically a small town.

"Well?" Orion prompted.

"Alex, set course for Pasadena and swing by a gas station." I sighed, leaning back into my seat. "We're gonna need some caffeine."

Pasadena is a part of East LA that's famous for being kind of normal. It's where people go to retire and live as close to the suburban life as you can get in the city limits. It's got big streets, large front yards, and a *chill* vibe. They filmed *Back to the Future* there. You can see the house—someone lives there.

As we made our way to Backus Avenue, I couldn't help but wonder how many supernatural beings lurked on these calm streets. Even immortals might want to retire eventually. What better way to do it than in the land of eternal summer among the palm trees?

"That's it," Alex called as he drove past the address. He didn't slow down, because we're professionals. This wasn't the first time that we had loaded into his minivan to break into a suburban home at night. I could only hope that it went better for us than usual, but the way everything had gone so far didn't leave me with much hope.

The house was exactly what I expected to find on this street. A pleasant two-story Tudor complete with a dark roof and white shutters. It had probably been built in the 1960s and lovingly maintained ever since. There was a dim light in the front window, but otherwise it was dark.

We continued halfway down the block before Alex pulled over and parked in front of a random house, then killed the engine. We lurked in the darkness for a few minutes, watching the street. As far as I could tell, there was nothing out of the ordinary, besides the demigod that lived in the neighborhood.

Eventually even Orion's patience ran thin. The Oracle's words hung over all of us like a threat, and I could tell he was chafing to do something about it.

"Let's go," he ordered, sliding open the back door with a vicious wrench.

We piled out of the van to walk at a brisk pace across the street and down the block toward Harmony's house. The weight of the pistol shoved down my back waistband demanded my attention. Bringing weapons to a neighborhood felt just as wrong this time as it had the last. In the distance, a dog barked, which felt like an ill omen.

Orion paused at the edge of the sidewalk that led up to Harmony's front door. The three of us froze, like a wolf pack waiting to pounce. I knew the Hunter was straining his hearing, listening for anything out of place. In the harsh shadows cast by streetlights, I saw a deep frown grow on his face. I was glad that it was dark out—it made the sword hilt peeking over Orion's right shoulder far less noticeable from a distance.

"Come," he growled, surging back into motion down the walkway. Together we mounted the wooden porch and paused at the door.

"Do we knock?" I murmured, keeping my voice low.

Orion shrugged and rapped his fist against it. A thrill of fear ran down my spine as the door slowly swung open, revealing a broken latch. The three of us exchanged knowing looks. If this Harmony woman was on the killer's list, the Piper might be here at this very moment. As one, we drew our pistols, Orion's relentless training taking over.

The Hunter took point while Alex and I trailed him, acting as the back corners of our triangle. Together we stepped into the front hall of the house, weapons drawn, angled down slightly.

The first thing I noticed was that the long, narrow rug in the hallway was twisted up on itself as if something had been dragged across it.

Alex turned to cover the living room to the left as we pushed in. I turned right to check an empty dining room. Orion continued forward like an arrow hurtling at its target. Confident that our flank was empty, I followed, covering wherever the point man wasn't looking.

We were all the way to the kitchen in the center of the home before I realized that my training had made me forget to be nervous. The moment we entered the home, my brain had stopped thinking and started only doing.

I'd come a long way since my first home raid, but I didn't

have time to pat myself on the back. In the back of the house, a woman shouted in pain. The room exploded into action as the Hunter surged forward, and I raced in his footsteps.

We shot through a door in the kitchen into the garage. It was empty and dark, except for a single pool of light in the center of its cement floor. A woman was strapped to a metal chair, bleeding from a cut on her forehead.

"Please! Help me!" she screamed as we burst into the room.

A second woman stood above her, dressed in black tactical gear. She spun at the sound of our entrance, and in the dim light I could just make out the lines of the Siren's tattoo around her right eye. She held a long white object that had to be her flute. My heart leapt as I realized this was who we had been looking for. The Pied Piper was here.

Time for some payback.

There was just enough time to see a flash of outraged surprise on the killer's face before everything went sideways. The black-clad woman didn't hesitate, diving into the darker corner of the garage.

Orion raised his pistol and fired, tracking her roll with calm competency. At that range there was no way he missed, but depending on the creature we were dealing with, bullets might not be enough to put her down for long.

I stepped to the side, clearing my line of fire. As my finger began to tighten on the trigger, something hammered my mind with the force of a freight train. It felt like I was standing on the beach as a tidal wave came crashing down on me.

My world went white.

Slowly, things began to return. I stood in a field of rolling hills that flowed as far as my eye could see. The bright sun shone down on me, and a playful breeze teased me, carrying the faint sounds of a distant, beautiful song. A smile stretched across my face as I turned in a circle, taking in my surroundings. It felt good to be home. I had missed this place.

But this wasn't my home.

For a second the world faltered, and the sun dimmed as if a cloud had passed across its face.

Oh yes, it was. What was I thinking?

I was late for something; I couldn't seem to remember what it was. It wasn't important what it was, only that I needed to be there. I set off at a brisk walk, making my way through the fields. Somehow I knew this was the way I needed to go.

I made it a dozen feet before the world around me rippled. Startled, I paused mid-stride. It was if someone had dropped a stone into a lake, but instead of water, the lake was the very air around me. I watched in confused fascination as more and more stones dropped, sending waves of oscillating rings throughout my reality.

Where was I trying to go? Wasn't I already somewhere I needed to be? Hadn't I been doing something important? I glanced down at my right hand. It was empty, but I could swear I felt a weight there.

Hadn't I just been holding a gun?

With a thought, the vision of the world around me shattered, and reality came flooding back in. I was back in Harmony's house. Well, I had never left, despite what my mind had seen. I had somehow made my way through the kitchen and halfway to the front hall.

Fear gripped me as I realized that I must have been hit with the same Siren's song that had killed those Nephilim. I spun, rushing back into the kitchen, terrified of what I would find waiting in the garage. The psychic attack from the flute had sent me to a field of rainbows, but I was hoping that wasn't what the people who died had seen.

Much to my relief, I found Alex going through the cabinets. His mouth was hanging open, a tiny bit of drool drizzling out the corner. His blue eyes were glazed and unfocused.

"Alex!" I snapped, shouting at him. My friend twitched, as if slightly bothered by my intrusion, but he didn't stop searching.

"Alex!" I shouted again.

"Hungry," he murmured in his dreamlike trance. He pulled a box of pancake mix from one of the cupboards and placed it on the counter. That told me he was *for sure* under the influence of the Piper's song. Alex was a waffle guy.

The sound of gunshots came from the garage, and I found that oddly reassuring. That meant Orion was still on his feet, doing battle with the killer. Alex twitched in time with the bullets, as if they were somehow disrupting the dreamland he was stuck in.

Of course.

The ripples I had seen flowing over my world had actually been waves. Sonic waves from Orion's gunshots, interfering with the sound of the song. It had been a lake, but a musical one.

Magic is cool, but science is crazy.

To snap Alex out of his trance, all I had to do was make enough noise to drown out the flute's music. Which, now that I thought about it, seemed sort of obvious. Regardless, we were in luck. I have never been accused of being particularly quiet.

Turning from my friend, I rooted through the cabinets myself, grabbing the first metal pot I found. Tucking it under my arm like a marching band drum, I fished through the drawers until I found a wooden spoon. Then I performed a drum solo that would have made three-year-old me seethe with jealousy.

With each bang on the pot, my friend twisted, as if noticing the sound waves crashing down on his world like a storm. Desperate to push him over the edge, I screamed a shrill cry of terror, banging as fast as I could.

"Ah, okay, okay! I'm back!" Alex shouted, abruptly jumping away from my performance. He shook his head like a dog and stared down at the box of mix on the counter.

"Pancakes?" he asked in a horrified tone.

More gunshots came from the garage.

"Later!" I shouted, turning from him and racing back toward Orion. I could hear Alex's feet pounding behind me as we burst into the middle of a war zone.

The Hunter's sword was in his hand. The straight blade was wreathed in a furious red fire that cast a warm glow throughout the room, banishing all shadows. This wasn't a garage at all, I realized, looking around. It was more of a workshop.

Harmony, whom I presumed was the woman tied to the chair, lay on her back, still bound. She let out a panicked whimper but could not flee. In the far corner of the room, the blond woman with the face tattoo had changed. Poisonous green scales decorated her face, and her jaw had opened wide to reveal teeth too long and sharp to be human. She was bleeding from a few holes that steamed where cold iron bullets—forged to hunt supernatural creatures like her—burned her flesh. But she was on her feet and seemed depressingly game for a fight.

With her left hand, she pointed a gun at the fallen form of Harmony. In her right, she grasped the pipe that was central to her branding. Now that I got a good look at it, it was the weirdest instrument I had ever seen. I almost suspected it hadn't originally been meant to be a flute. It was entirely white, with a lump on either end like a cap. A series of finger holes had been drilled down the long center.

"Surrender," Orion ordered, holding the blade in an extended guard toward the cornered woman.

"Never," she hissed. Her sharp teeth added vitriol to her words.

"You came to my city and killed my people. I do not know what you hoped to find, but you have found me. I do not know who you work for, but they will not save you." The Hunter took one step toward her.

"You cannot stop me, Hunter. I came for revenge on those who dared to keep my mother a prisoner on her island. But you are on my list. You will pay the price for her murder."

I let out a gasp of surprise. Even Orion froze, caught off guard. I had assumed that the Pied Piper was working for some collector. It hadn't occurred to me that she might be a daughter of the Siren. I guess that made sense. Everyone else in the supernatural world seemed to have offspring. Why not Peisinoe? Maybe some of those shipwrecked sailors had made it to the island after all.

"What is your name?" Orion demanded after a moment of shock.

"I am Clarissa, daughter of Peisinoe, Heir of the Siren. I will destroy my mother's enemies and claim her legacy. Not even you will keep me from it." The creature's eyes, a deep green to match her scales, flashed with rage. As Orion lunged forward, she raised the flute to her lips a second time and blew with tremendous force.

I was running down a long, dark hallway.

In the distance, a *thing* followed in my wake. It was relentless, tireless. I could only make out its white teeth and eyes. The rest was merely a blacker shadow against the darkness that surrounded me as it flowed after me like smoke.

Panic filled me, consuming my reason. I was incapable of forming thoughts. All I knew was that if I slowed down even for a moment, the thing that followed would rend me limb from limb. With a roar like a lion, the creature charged me, white eyes burning with bright light.

Screaming, I dove out of the creature's way. I felt the wind of its passing as it raced by. I turned to watch it in time to see another one of the beasts barreling toward me from the opposite direction. It wasn't just one. There was a whole pack!

I barely managed to scramble to my feet and dive out of the oncoming monster's path before it shot past. It was so heavy that it shook my whole world. There was a distant sound of trumpets, and for a second everything went blurry.

Shaking my head to clear it, I felt my stomach drop as I saw a dozen pairs of white eyes coming toward me in three lines. They were everywhere! Whatever these creatures were, they didn't seem to be able to turn quickly. I managed to leap out of their path and watched with bated breath as they hurtled by.

Each time I dodged one, my world shook with its passing.

I was so caught up in dodging the line of oncoming beasts, I didn't notice that another of the bastards had managed to creep up behind me. I screamed and dove to the side, landing on my stomach on something hard. It let out a roar as it barreled down on me.

I was lying on a concrete sidewalk.

My stomach and elbows screamed in pain from the hard landing we'd just taken. Slowly, I pushed myself up to a sitting position and turned to stare at the freeway I had just crossed in numb disbelief.

The white eyes of the monsters had been headlights and the roars their horns as drivers tried to chase me off the road. I let out a shaky laugh as I sat there on the side of the road. I didn't trust my legs to stand. My whole body was shaking with fear as I stared at the six lanes of traffic that I had just thrown myself through.

For a long time, I remained there, watching the cars pass by as I tried to collect my wits. Where were Alex and Orion? We had all been in the room when the woman had blown her terrible flute once more. It occurred to me that Clarissa wasn't as good at this as her mother had allegedly been.

Based on how supernatural powers work, that would make sense from a DNA standpoint. If her mother was the sole Siren, then Clarissa could only be half Siren at best. That would make her half as effective as her mother.

I had a new level of appreciation for Odysseus, tied to his ship's mast, hit with the full force of a true Siren's song. No wonder so many ships had crashed on those horrible rocks. The only reason I wasn't dead was because the cars had made enough noise to shatter the song's illusion.

I eyed a rumbling eighteen-wheeler as it careened past me at fifty miles an hour. If this was a Siren at half power, I was only too glad I hadn't been there when Orion killed the original model.

WHEN MY LEGS were solid enough to support me, I staggered to my feet and headed back. This journey was much safer, since I used the crosswalk and waited for the white light to tell me when to go.

According to my phone's map, I had traversed three blocks in whatever fugue state Clarissa had put me in. I traced my way back to the house at a sprint, worrying about my friends. I had been lucky enough to survive my brush with the deadly song, but that didn't mean we all had.

Those Nephilim at Dardan's house had died.

I swallowed my fear and doubled my pace, barreling down

the quiet suburban street like it was a racetrack. I kicked something heavy as I ran, causing me to stumble. Cursing over my stubbed toe, I bent to scoop up my missing pistol. Relief flooded through me as I felt the weapon's weight in my hand. Orion wouldn't have let me live it down if I had lost this. I checked the magazine and was pleased to find it was still loaded—I hadn't tried to shoot any of the monsters chasing me in my vision.

I found Alex first.

The younger Nephilim was climbing the large Spanish oak tree in Harmony's front yard. He was shirtless, for some reason, and screamed in fury as he swung a branch like a sword at enemies I couldn't see.

"Alex!" I shouted, staring up at him almost two stories above me. "Be careful!" My friend twitched as my voice tangled with the earworm that Clarissa's flute had placed in his mind. But he continued his climb up the limbs like a pirate on the mast.

"Dude, you gotta get down!" I let out a curse as I raced toward the base of the tree. I wasn't really sure what my plan was. If I could even climb high enough to reach him, there was a very good chance he would see me as another enemy and attack. At that height we could both fall and break our backs. It would only be too ironic if Clarissa failed to kill me with her song, but I then died to the one she gave Alex. Despite it all, I didn't hesitate to start climbing. He'd do the same for me. That's how the Hunt works.

Gritting my teeth, I jumped and grabbed one of the lowest branches, pulling myself up into the tree. This was such a bad idea. I stood on the limb and reached for the next one, which was thankfully closer. Bit by bit I levered myself up after my shirtless friend. The tree was old and thick, but it still shook as the spry Nephilim leapt around, dueling imaginary foes.

When I was over a story high, still trailing after my song-struck friend, Harmony's front door slammed open. I let out a squawk of surprise and caught myself before I fell from the branch I was sitting on as Orion burst out into the night. I could just make out his black hair sticking wildly in every direction and his wide-eyed face in the low light. He looked like he had just woken up.

He took in the scene at a glance, his brows furrowing at the sight of his two squires climbing a tree with only one shirt between the two of us. "Alex!" he snapped with a voice of command. It wasn't particularly loud, but it was sharp.

My friend let out a gasp of surprise, like a man jolting out of a nightmare, and then a scream of terror as he realized he was dangling from the top of an oak tree. "What the hell?" he demanded, wrapping himself around the trunk.

"Seems Siren Junior turned you into a pirate and tried to make you walk the plank," I called up at him, a chuckle bursting out of my chest. I was relieved to see both of my friends alive and well. Orion glowered up at us from the base of the tree.

"Honestly? It was kind of fun," Alex remarked from above.

"Lucky." I dropped to a lower branch before letting myself fall all the way to the ground. "I got put on the highway. Almost got run over." I glanced over at our boss, who was watching Alex's descent with the irritation of a homeowner who's caught the neighborhood kids playing in his yard. "What happened to you?"

"I fell asleep," he grunted.

"That's it?" I asked incredulously.

He shrugged as if to say, *What do you expect?* Which was a fair question. In fact, now that I thought about it, Clarissa's attack had seemed to affect each of us differently. Out of all the members of the Hunt, only I had ended up in traffic, almost run over. Alex had been in danger of breaking some bones or maybe his neck in a bad fall. But comparatively, climbing a tree was not nearly as dangerous as playing in the middle of a freeway. Orion falling asleep was barely worth mentioning.

I sincerely doubted that it was a coincidence that our resistance to the visions of the flute seemed to correspond to the amount of demon blood flowing in our veins. As the token mortal of the organization, I'd taken the full force of the instrument's power. Alex had enough supernatural DNA to weaken it, and it had practically bounced off Orion.

Yet another reminder of the inherent weakness of my body compared with the predators all around me. I sighed in frustration but tried not to let it settle into my chest. There was nothing I could do about it; might as well focus on what I could affect.

But that begged the question, why was I still alive? The Nephilim we had seen earlier today had all died to the Piper's song. Why did they die when I lived? I frowned, trying to come up with a good reason. Clarissa seemed to operate like an assassin, sneaking up on her victims. But tonight, we ambushed her, catching her off guard. Maybe she wasn't as good a player when she was on her back foot? It was a halfway decent theory. Something to keep in mind for the future.

"Harmony and the Piper?" I asked Orion as Alex dropped down to join us.

"Oh, my shirt," the smaller man announced, bending over to pick something up off the ground. I wondered what exactly he had seen that made him feel like he needed to take that off before he started climbing, but I decided not to ask.

"Gone when I came to," the Constellation almost snarled. That might be a major contributor to his bad mood. Not only had our quarry slipped through our hands, but she had kidnapped another Nephilim. Worse—we still didn't know *why* she was doing this.

"Well," I replied slowly as Alex—now shirted—joined us. "Time to work the crime scene?"

"Quickly," Alex urged, glancing at our simmering boss. "The cops will be here soon."

"That was a lot of bullets," I agreed. I glanced down the street at the rest of the previously sleepy neighborhood. All of the lights were out except for the ones in Harmony's home, casting the entire block into a deep darkness. I could practically feel the tension of the people who sheltered there, waiting for the danger to pass.

I felt a little guilty. We hadn't brought the violence here. But the advent of the Hunt is never a good sign for safety or property values. At least no mortals were hurt. Excluding me and my road rash, I guess.

Orion led us back into the home at a brisk trot. Once inside, we split up to scan the place for clues. It sounds very Scooby-Doo-ish, but what else could we do? These weren't random crimes; the Siren's spawn was up to something. She had practically told us that herself.

I made my way back into the workshop where the fight had gone down. Flicking on the light, my eyes widened as I took in what had been an immaculate studio. Woodworking tools hung from the wall, each in a spot made just for it. I could tell that the room had been someone's safe space, their quiet little laboratory away from the world.

Now it had too many bullet holes in the walls.

On a long, low table were various projects clamped down by vises. To the left was a framed sheet of music, the paper old and yellow. I glanced at it, but the few words in the margins seemed to be in German, and I am a victim of the American education system, so I didn't have a clue what it might say.

There was an old-fashioned secretary's desk, one of those covered ones where a half circle of wood comes down from the top like a convertible's roof to protect everything within. It was secured with a small lock where the bottom of the lid met the top of the desk.

Alex had been teaching me to pick locks, and given enough time, I probably could have finessed my way through this one. But we were on the clock. Glancing at the wall, I grabbed one of Harmony's power tools—an immaculately stored electric hand-saw—and set it against the wood. Before I turned it on, I realized I had forgotten something important. I grabbed a pair of large plastic glasses from the workshop table and slid them on my face.

Never hurts to be safe.

The wood shell was surprisingly thick, but the saw was powerful. Splinters flew everywhere as I sheared my way through the covering. The whole thing shifted with a *pop* as I severed the connection between the lock and the rest of the shell.

I dropped the power tool back on the worktable and turned to find Orion lurking in the doorway. I jumped in surprise; I hadn't heard him over the sound of the cutting. He arched an eyebrow at my demolition project but didn't say anything. He's the kind of teacher that likes to let his students fail all the way before he gives feedback.

So I turned away, lifting the lid to rifle through the papers on the desk. The first stack contained a bunch of pencil drawings. As I flipped through them, I realized they weren't artworks but design sketches, each for an exquisite musical instrument.

I paused in surprise and turned to scan the room again. I hadn't paid much attention to *what* the projects on the table had been, but now that I looked, it was obvious that they were instruments mid-construction. That curved thing in the center was some sort of violin—or maybe a viola? Does anyone actually know what the difference is? The one on the left I was pretty sure going to become a guitar. Some eluded me, but the last one was easy enough to identify. It was going to be a flute.

Dread ran through me as I realized this was a master instrument maker's workshop. That couldn't be a coincidence. The daughter of the long-dead Siren, who possessed a flute that could wield some of her mother's power, wasn't just randomly kidnapping a woman who could make or maybe improve instruments.

"Uh-oh," I breathed.

"Time to go!" Alex called, appearing behind Orion's shoulder. "I can hear sirens—well, the police kind, not—you get it."

On a hunch, I tucked the stack of sketches under my arm and ran to follow the rest of the Hunt out of the house. The cop cars were close enough that even my mortal ears could hear them wailing as they raced toward Harmony's house.

We dove into Alex's van and at Orion's direction set off deeper into the neighborhood. I leaned back in the front seat, using my phone's light to study the sketches further. I'd have been more nervous if this were our first time running from the police through the suburbs. They weren't going to catch us; our guy literally *invented* hunting prey. His instincts would be more than enough for us to evade notice.

I'd flipped through Harmony's entire catalog by the time we made it back onto the 110. We all relaxed as we joined the late-night traffic heading back into LA proper. I'm no musician, and I'm not particularly handy. Most of my teachers described me as "mouthy," which is a very different vibe. But from what I could tell, the descendant of the Muse was extremely talented. I guess it ran in her family. Each sketch depicted an instrument that was beyond ornamental; it looked like it would have been at home in a king's personal collection. Plus, it was impressive that she could design different types. I suspect the skill set required to make a violin is entirely different from the one needed for a trumpet. Strings and brass are different things, after all.

"What are you studying?" Orion called to me, now that he was no longer directing our escape. "It's not like you to be quiet this long."

"I'm not sure," I admitted, flipping back and forth between designs for a particularly ornate cello and a mandolin that looked like it was supposed to be made almost entirely of silver. "But it looks like Harmony was some sort of instrument maker."

"That's oddly specific," Alex commented after a moment of silence. "A woman with a powerful magical flute kidnaps someone who can make instruments?"

"That's what I'm thinking too," I told him. "But that's sort of just a guess. I know detectives on TV shows don't like the idea of coincidences, but this is real life. We've got magic and Fae running around. Surely coincidences could exist too, right?"

"I don't believe in them," Orion interjected gruffly from the back.

"Okay, that's a no." I sighed, tucking the sketches into Alex's glove box for safekeeping. "So then we assume the obvious, I guess. The Piper's flute isn't as powerful as it could be, and she wants the instrument maker to upgrade it for her."

"Not that strong?" Alex objected in mild outrage. "It made me climb a tree!"

"Shirtless," I reminded him.

"Exactly." He sounded a little embarrassed.

"But that's it. I know she used it to make the guards turn on one another at the warehouse, but she didn't manage to kill any of us. Heck, it only managed to knock Orion out," I pointed out. "There's got to be some limits on it. Boss man, how does the flute compare with the original song? The legend of the Pied Piper leading all those rats and kids away sounds about right, but I'm guessing that's a fraction of what a Siren could do."

"It is a grain of sand next to an entire beach," the Hunter confirmed.

"That's what I thought," I grunted, my sense of unease growing.

"But we know she can kill with it," Alex pointed out.

"My gut says it's because we caught her off guard," I told them, thinking of my earlier theory. "She probably snuck up on Dardan and the other Nephilim, so they didn't fight back. Almost like carbon monoxide."

"But Lazarus's guards were also Nephilim, and they weren't ambushed," Alex pointed out.

"True." I frowned, trying to figure out how that fit. "But she didn't kill them with the song itself. She made them kill one another."

"And maybe she had that particular tune ready to go, instead of having to compose something off the top of her head when we jumped her."

"It's a theory." I looked down at the sketches in my hands again.

I felt a sense of satisfaction unraveling the twisty knots of this plot. I'd only been aware of the supernatural world for four months, but I felt I was finally coming into my own. The old me, the sad one who had given up, would never have thought I could do something like this. Now it felt almost as natural as breathing—which, by the way, I was lucky to still be doing.

"Orion," I began as a new idea struck me, "what do you know about the other Nephilim? Dardan and the others she killed before. Also, why did she kidnap Harmony but not any of them?"

"Yeah, that is a really good point," Alex replied. "That doesn't seem to fit our idea."

"I do not know much about the younger ones," Orion mused after a few moments of thought. "But Dardan, the elder, was a descendant of Osiris."

Because I'm an idiot who can't be expected to remember more than the most famous demigods, I pulled out my phone and typed in a quick search for the Nephilim's ancestor. A frown grew on my face as I began to read.

"Hey, guys," I said slowly, still scrolling through the article. "Osiris's family line is tied to death, and specifically to a tradition that put a lot of emphasis on the care of a body after death."

"You're talking about how the ancient Egyptians would mummify people?" Alex asked.

"Yeah," I replied, setting down my phone to think. That felt like another thing that couldn't be a coincidence. Clarissa had said she was here to "claim her mother's legacy" and had stolen the long-lost remains of her mother's body after killing a Nephilim who had something to do with preparing dead bodies.

What was I missing?

Something blindingly obvious, probably.

"Dardan died hours after the other Nephilim. What if Clarissa didn't need him to do something for her, but she did need him to teach her something?" I shivered at thought of being interrogated by the Pied Piper for hours.

"Like what?" Alex asked.

I frowned, trying to follow the dim outline of an idea lurking in my mind. "We're not worried about resurrection, right?" I asked the car. "That's not a thing that could be happening here?" I didn't think so, but it felt smart to cross it off the list.

"Even if it were possible, her head is still in a volcano," Orion reminded me with grim satisfaction. Okay, that was a good point. I don't know anything about bringing dead things to life, but it does seem like wasted effort if they immediately die again because they don't have a head.

So the Siren really was dead and not coming back. Then what possible use could—my thoughts derailed as inspiration struck. There was something different about the flute. I had just assumed that it was old and weird. It was, I was right. But that's not all that it was.

I sat up in the chair as if I had been bitten and reached for the sketches in the glove box again. I flipped through until I found the design for a flute that I had passed by.

BONE FLUTE it said at the top of the page, in perfect handwriting.

"I know what she's trying to do," I told Orion.

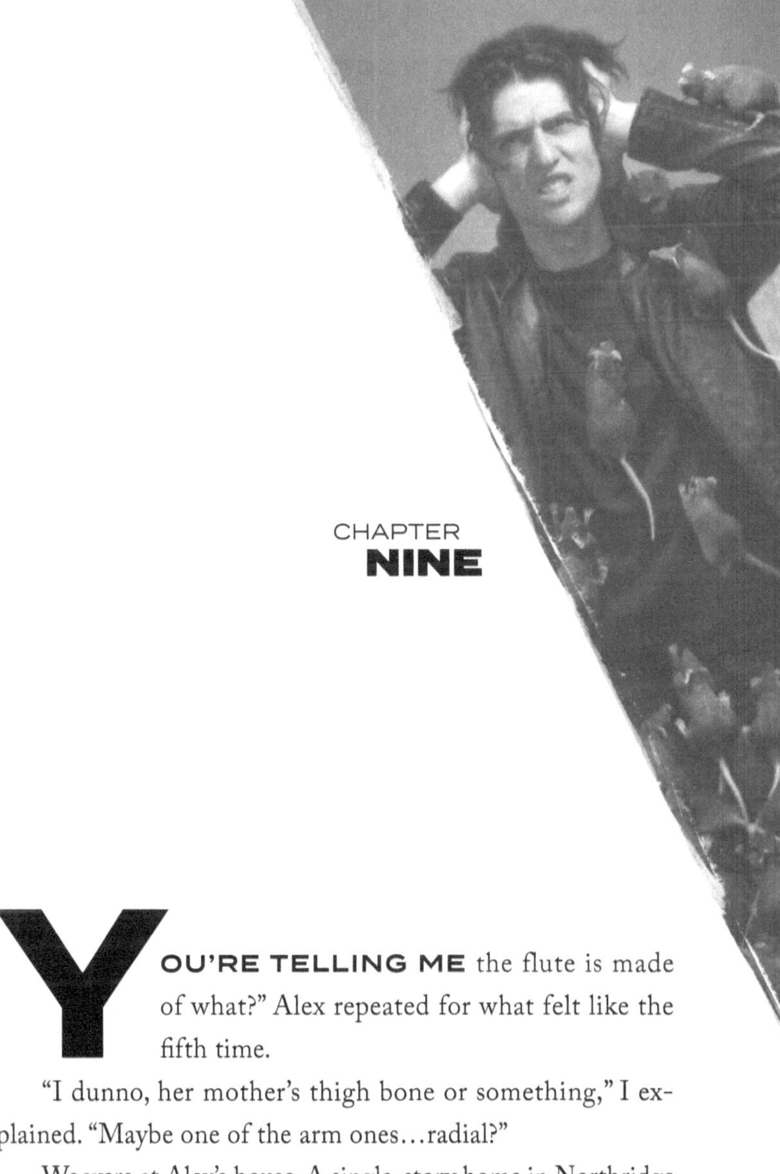

YOU'RE TELLING ME the flute is made of what?" Alex repeated for what felt like the fifth time.

"I dunno, her mother's thigh bone or something," I explained. "Maybe one of the arm ones…radial?"

We were at Alex's house. A single-story home in Northridge that could only be described as a bachelor pad, if the bachelor in question was two hundred years old and had spent most of that time single. Movie posters decorated the walls, along with swords from days long past. His couch had a towering stack of comic books next to it. They used to be on it, but these days I spend most of my nights on that sofa, to avoid a situation at home that is growing increasingly awkward.

"Where would she get one of the Siren's bones?" Alex challenged. "Orion threw her body in the sea."

"While we fought, I cut off one of her arms. I do not recall if I gathered it with the rest of her when I disposed of her corpse." Orion shrugged stiffly from where he lurked in the corner of the room, leaning against the wall with his arms crossed. He wore a larger scowl than usual, obviously annoyed at himself.

"Okay, walk me through this one more time," Alex asked, burying his head in his hands next to me at the dining room table.

"The flute is made out of bone—probably an arm bone. That's why it's white and has that weird flare on the end," I said, holding up my fingers to count the points on it. "It must let Clarissa channel some of her mother's power."

"For centuries she's only had Mommy Dearest's arm bone, so her ability to imitate has been limited," Alex continued, picking up where I left off. "But then Lazarus finds the rest of Peisinoe's body."

"Which means that she suddenly has a chance to get her hands on a freaking treasure trove of power," I agree. "But that's not enough. Any idiot can make a flute. She might have made it herself. That could be part of why her power is limited or inconsistent."

"She needs experts to craft weapons of higher quality for her." Orion's voice was grim, but his contribution meant that he approved of our theory. "Dardan taught her how to extricate the remains. Harmony is going to turn them into instruments."

"But she killed Dardan," Alex pointed out.

"Maybe that part is easier? Maybe it isn't *art*."

"Ah," Orion breathed in understanding after a moment. Art, as it has been explained to me, is mostly the domain of mortals. It's hard to make it if you don't have a soul. I'm not sure how someone in the Muse family tree fits into that rubric; maybe they get a special exception.

Clarissa needed Dardan's knowledge, and there was nothing stopping her from following his instructions. But I suspected that making high-quality musical instruments might fall outside of what she was able to do on her own. That's why she needed Harmony alive.

"Obviously this isn't just about power—it's some sort of revenge tour." I leaned back in my chair in thought. "You're on the list for obvious reasons, but she also said something about whoever kept her mother imprisoned on the island?"

"The gods," Orion grunted unhelpfully.

"The gods, got it. That is pretty general, do we have anything more specific? There are a lot of those, or so I hear."

"Well, they would be Greek," Alex pointed out.

"So…Zeus and company?"

Alex pulled out his phone and made a quick search. "According to this, Peisinoe was the daughter of a river god named Achelous and…one of the Muses." The room went still as we processed this information.

"You didn't think that was relevant?" I demanded from Orion.

He shrugged abashedly. "It has been a long time."

"If it matters, it's a completely different family of Muses from Harmony," Alex informed us, eyes still locked on his screen.

"Music needs Muses, I get it. Now she's going to use one to somehow hunt a god, and us."

"Okay, so we know what she's doing," Alex mused, leaning back in his chair. "But now the real question is what do we do with that? Clarissa kidnapped Harmony. She has her weapon maker and her material."

"So we find them." I looked toward the Hunter expectantly. "That seems like your department."

"I snagged a hairbrush." Alex lifted a plastic bag that indeed held a brush full of strands of Harmony's golden hair.

"Oh, dude, that's so smart," I said. I may have cracked the *why* of the case, but Alex had been incredibly practical. If you have a piece of someone—their hair or blood usually does the trick—it's easy to track them. "Fancy a tracking spell, boss?" I asked, turning to him.

Wordlessly, the big man began preparing the tracker. There was a reluctance to his actions that told me something was wrong. Maybe he was just beating himself up about leaving the Siren's arm behind. But how could he have known?

Despite being technically magic, the process of making a tracking spell is pretty boring. The Constellation took a baggie and filled it with some herbs, a strand of Harmony's hair, and some of his own blood. When he was done, he crammed the mixture into a corner of the bag and twisted it to form an arrow.

Then he placed the arrow in the palm of his flat hand and waited. Alex and I peered over his shoulder. If it worked, the bag would spin like a compass. The corner with all the stuff in it was supposed to point in the direction of the hair's owner.

"I don't suppose there's any chance that she's straight ahead?" I asked solemnly after the bag didn't move.

"She's being kept inside a circle," Orion grunted, tossing the bag to the tabletop with an annoyed grunt. "It was a good thought." He glanced at Alex, who looked crushed that his contribution hadn't worked. "But this foe is old and dangerous. She knows better than to make such a simple mistake."

"Then what do we do?" Alex asked, his tone dour. "We can't just wait for her to make more powerful weapons. She may not be here for you in particular, Orion, but you did kill her mother. I'm sure once she gets what she wants…"

"I know." He was quiet—a rare moment of hesitation. Which meant that he knew what we needed to do, but he didn't like it. Which meant we needed help, and there was only one place we could get that. I didn't like it either.

"We have to call Lazarus," I answered. The Hunter looked at me sharply. "We made an alliance to share information about this, and he might have a better way to track her." His black eyes bored into mine, but he didn't disagree. "What do you want me to tell him?" Once again, Constellations don't make their own phone calls.

"Tell him the truth," Orion sighed after a moment of thought. He had agreed, and his honor would not let him hold anything back. "Tell him who the Piper is and what we think she is trying to do."

I nodded, pulled out my phone, and dialed the number the mobster had given me. The line didn't even ring, just went from silence to a voice. "Hello, Mr. Carver," Lazarus said, his cultured tones ringing in my ears. "I can only assume that you have something interesting to share on behalf of your master?"

"Yeah, I got an update," I grumbled, rolling my eyes at Alex. "We tracked the Piper to the home of a Nephilim in Pasadena."

"Who?"

"Name's Harmony. She's a descendant of one of the Muses."

"Interesting."

"The Piper isn't a contractor," I told him, ignoring his tone. "She's the daughter of the Siren."

"You're sure?"

"She stated it rather proudly. Plus, we believe her flute is made out of one of her mother's arm bones."

The silence on the other side of the line was palpable. I don't like the guy, but that doesn't mean I think he's stupid. If anything, he's so smart that he can't feel things right. A man ruled by vicious logic, he sees the world the way a scientist sees an amoeba under a microscope.

I knew he was already processing the idea that Peisinoe's bones could be turned into weapons. Once that fully sank in, he'd do anything to get them back. That didn't seem like a good idea, but the decision was above my pay grade.

"What happened to this Harmony?"

"Clarissa—that's the Piper's real name—took her. She appears to be some sort of instrument maker." There was another prolonged silence. I could practically hear the gears of the old man's mind grinding through the phone.

"Well, that's less than ideal," he drawled eventually. "You assume that she plans to coerce the Museling to build her a more powerful weapon from her mother's remains?" See, this is exactly what I was talking about. It took us an hour to come up with this. He did it in twenty seconds.

"Yes."

"We should prevent that." Across the room, Orion nodded once. Just because he wasn't on the call didn't mean he couldn't hear what was being discussed.

"The Hunt agrees," I replied. "We need help locating her.

Then we're happy to take her down."

"I assume that you tried a tracking spell of some sort on Harmony?" The question was mild, but I found it a little insulting on Orion's behalf. No, man, the Hunter didn't think of that. What a great idea.

"She's hidden, so we assume they're in a circle."

"Very well. Mundane methods will have to suffice. Give me the address and time of the incident. My people will find them." I couldn't help but feel a chill at the calm confidence in his voice. The worst part was that I didn't doubt him in the slightest. I've seen enough of what goes on underneath the hood of his organization to believe that his resources are more robust than those of some countries.

Feeling more than a little creeped out, I gave him the information he'd asked for.

"It will take a bit of time for us to locate them. Be ready to move when I call," he instructed. Then the line went dead.

"I hate that guy," I announced as I tucked my phone away.

"Now what?" Alex asked.

"Get some rest," Orion ordered, levering himself off the wall where he had been brooding. Without another word, he went outside to brood some more. I assume that's what he does to rest... I'm not entirely sure that he *needs* sleep. Outside of Clarissa's lullaby, I've never seen him even take a nap. As a mortal, I actually need some shut-eye to function at my best—and my best is barely better than his worst.

With a grunt, I dropped onto the sofa and idly picked up one of Alex's comic books. The heroes appeared to be fighting some villains with a sonic blast attack that would drive them to their knees. I snorted in sympathy. There was nothing fun about that experience. But as I read about superhumans struggling against sound waves, I realized that we still had a problem.

Even after Lazarus and his people found where Clarissa had stashed Harmony, we were the ones who'd have to go get her out. Which meant that we'd also have to square up against the Piper's musical attacks once more. Last time we'd caught her off guard, but we couldn't count on that now. Also, I had no idea how long it might take to turn a supernatural creature's bones into a fancy musical weapon. But if she had one by the time we found her, it could be a problem.

Orion wasn't worried—all she had managed to do was make him pass out for a moment. Compared with what her mother could do, that was barely a blip on the radar. But if the Hunter can be accused of having a fault, it's maybe reckless confidence.

When you're over a millennium old and no one has managed to kill you yet, I can't imagine you spend much time worrying about it anymore. I, on the other hand, was only twenty-four, and people kept getting way too close to murdering me for my comfort.

"What are we going to do about our hearing?" I asked Alex, looking up from the comic.

"Our Achilles' heel," my friend grunted, shifting to look at me.

"Boss doesn't seem too worried, but..."

"When does he?"

"Exactly. And if it's all the same to everyone, I'd prefer to keep my shirt on."

"That's because you don't have a six-pack as good as mine." Alex waved his hand over his shoulder, brushing imaginary flowing locks away in a haughty gesture.

"I also don't have demon blood," I grumbled, promising myself I'd start doing more crunches. Any day now, I'd get around to them. "The point is, you and I were more susceptible to the Piper's powers even without an upgrade. If she has enough time to get Harmony to tinker with her flute before we get there…"

"Then I might end up with no pants on."

"And nobody wants that."

"Ain't that the truth," my friend sighed.

Together, we rooted through one of Alex's closets full of random things until we found the best solution we could come up with. It was a Frankenstein collection of sound dampeners, cobbled together to try to achieve a perfect level of deafness.

I jammed in a set of squishy plugs—the kind you smush down, and then they inflate to fill your entire ear canal. It felt super weird, but it definitely reduced my ability to hear. Over that, I ran a pair of small over-ear wireless headphones that were connected to my phone. I could pump them full of white noise to overwhelm my brain's ability to hear anything else. On the top of this monstrosity, I placed a pair of oversized shooting-range headphones that had built-in noise cancellation.

"You look ridiculous," Alex said, looking at me.

"What?" I replied. My friend twitched in surprise, and I realized I had to be shouting.

"I guess that means it works," he sighed.

"I guess that means it works!" I told him. Alex rolled his eyes for some reason as I began dismantling my ear protection.

"Honestly, once you know the Siren's deal, she doesn't seem that powerful," I mused, stacking all my supplies by the couch in case I needed them in a hurry. "Like, what is she supposed to do if you can't hear her?"

"I think that's what all the teeth were for."

Why do they always have to have teeth?

I **WAS WRESTLING WITH** the iron bands of an anaconda when the keen wail of a ringtone cut through my dreams. Gasping and dripping with sweat, I sat up on Alex's couch, tangled in the deadly coils of my blanket. Sunlight streamed in through the slats of the blinds, and I reached for my ringing phone.

"This is Matt," I grumbled, answering it.

"So sorry to wake you," Lazarus replied acerbically. "But some of us have been working." I'm not a morning person; I think that anyone who has ever met me knows this. My brain doesn't start working until it's been out of dreamland for a little while. I had no clever little comeback loaded in the chamber for the old man, so I chose to ignore his barb.

"Did you find her?" I asked, my voice still rough.

"Yes." He hesitated for a moment. "Up to a point."

"What do you mean, 'up to a point'?"

"She's gone underground. But I know where the entrance to her lair is. The rest will be up to the skills of the Hunt."

"What do you mean, 'underground'?" I asked incredulously. "Where could you even go underground here? This isn't New York. We have too many earthquakes."

He told me.

"Oh for crying out loud," I breathed.

"We are monitoring all the exits, but they have not emerged. Which means…"

"Which means someone gets to go in and find her," I grumbled.

One of the most iconic sites in this city is a massive ditch rather ironically called the Los Angeles River. It *is* technically a river—or used to be. I don't know if it still qualifies. Now it's more of a gravestone marking the water that used to exist in this desert. Ninety percent of the time it's bone-dry, a massive concrete expanse with bridges running over it. It's used to catch the runoff from the flash floods we get when it does rain. During those brief periods it will fill up as all the water that falls on the entire city rushes there like a mosh pit.

It's featured in every 1990s action movie set in LA. Somehow every hero ends up in a car chase driving through its empty culverts and along the tiny little stream that flows most of the time. But that's not all that's in the riverbed.

We may not have subway tunnels here, but we have plenty of sewer ones. Massive storm drains pull water in and funnel it into waste treatment plants, aquifers, and wherever else rainwater goes. Lazarus and a couple of his operators were waiting for us at the entrance of one, underneath a bridge that connects to the Arts District to Downtown. They came in a pair of matching black vans, but there was a third car parked by the entrance, a gray sedan that looked like it hadn't been here long.

Clarissa the Pied Piper had taken her prey into the water tunnels; maybe she'd learned about them from the rats she'd led away so long ago. Now that she was underground, she and Harmony were hidden from the cameras and satellites Lazarus's people had used to track her movements. They knew she was in there, but they had no idea where.

We met at the back of one of their Sprinter vans, where half a dozen armed Nephilim in tactical gear stood behind the old man. All of them eyed Orion warily, but their assault rifles dangled in slings rather than resting in their hands, so their glares lacked much punch.

"What's with the dogs?" Alex jerked his hands at the operators. One woman with short dark hair sneered in his direction, but my friend ignored them.

"They're here to protect my investment," Lazarus replied evenly.

"Investment?" Orion rumbled.

"This Clarissa stole her mother's bones from me. They are mine by right, and when the day is done and the people saved, my men will collect them."

Alex and I exchanged nervous glances out of the corners of our eyes. "I'm not sure—"

"This was the agreement, Mr. Carver," Lazarus replied, not breaking eye contact with Orion. "Both of us were wronged, and we have allied to make these wrongs right. To do anything else would be a gesture of bad faith."

Orion shrugged in bored acceptance, but I could tell he was seething. His spine was too straight, shoulders too rigid. He's the kind of man who burns cold. The angrier he gets, the more he resembles an icicle.

"Well, we have done our part." Lazarus gestured at the yawing storm drain entrance waiting for us. "Now hunt." His lips quirked in a dry smile.

Before we entered, Alex and I strapped on our sound protection. My three layers of noise insulation felt like a suit of armor, and as Orion took his first step into the dark, I wasn't that worried. That feeling faded as we got farther in. It was just beyond creepy in there. Absolute dark is something I only want to see what when I'm under the covers, trying to sleep. The only monsters in my room are the ones under my bed, and I stopped being afraid of them a long time ago.

But in an underground tunnel network that has *real* monsters in it, the crushing black was terrifying. I'd never seen anything like it. LA is a city of light pollution, and even with blackout curtains I'd never managed to get my room this dark. It was what the void of space must be like.

Alex and I both carried assault rifles equipped with flashlights, which we used to sweep the tunnels as we crept through them. Orion merely drew his sword as he walked into the dark. The blade's bright fire blazed like a beacon, pushing back the crushing night that surrounded us.

Although LA had been rainless for a while, the tunnels were damp and moldy. I couldn't hear anything, but I could feel the puddles that I stepped in, and I just *knew* that eerie little drips echoed through the concrete maze. It was the creepiest place I had ever been. Orion led our group, and I made sure to keep an eye on him for hand signals. The Hunter hadn't bothered wearing any ear protection, but he had approved of both of his squires shielding up.

Maybe a hundred yards in, we reached an intersection, and the Hunter dropped into a crouch. Holding his blade close to the ground, he frowned as he studied the mud, looking for signs. I shined my light down on the center, trying to help illuminate any tracks. After a moment Orion pointed one long finger at a fresh-looking divot that might have been from a boot before rising.

Without looking back, he strode through the rightmost tunnel, following the trail he had indicated. Alex and I walked in his wake, weapons at the ready. The white noise piping in through my headphones was starting to feel like it was the static of my own brain. I couldn't hear myself think, which, depending on who you ask, might have been an improvement.

We journeyed through another long tunnel. In my mind it felt like we were sloping downward, as if each step was taking us deeper into the foundations of the earth. Realistically, we were probably only twenty or thirty feet below the surface, but in the dark it felt like much more.

This truly was a place for a monster to lair.

I wondered if Clarissa was the only thing to take up residence down here. I'd heard tales of the alligators that lurk in New York sewers. Why not vampires or monsters? No sooner had that thought occurred to me than I was sure it was right. Where else would they be but here?

We entered another open area, and Orion stiffened. He

raised his left hand and clenched it into a fist. Alex and I froze in his shadow. I raised my rifle to point forward, while my friend turned to cover our back, as we had agreed. I could feel my pulse pounding as I stared down the sights. The bubble of white noise that I was trapped in only made everything more terrifying. Without one of my most important senses, I didn't know how scared I was supposed to be. So I became terrified, just in case.

I could see the light of my rifle shaking in my hands, but I remembered the Hunter's lessons and exhaled, trying to get control. Ahead of me Orion tapped his ear, then made the signal we had devised for music before he pointed forward.

He heard the Piper.

My heart began to race as I stared into the gloom beyond the edge of the sword's glow. Suddenly it felt like the void was peering back into me. My skin crawled as I imagined a thousand tiny eyes staring at me, unseen in the dark.

Guided by my fear, I swept the light on my weapon from side to side and twitched as I caught a flutter of movement on the edge of my beam. I tightened my grip on my weapon, snapping to the left, following the motion.

A pair of beady eyes stared back at me, gleaming in the dark. My heart skipped a beat, but after a moment I relaxed. It was only a rat. New York was famous for the rats in its sewers, and apparently LA was no slouch in that department either. This sucker was pretty big. I let out a small sigh and relaxed my grip on the rifle.

"It's just a rat!" I called, pointing at the little vermin.

The rodent stared at us with calm curiosity, like it had never seen humans before. I don't have a lot of experience with wild rats, but I know they're smart. This one didn't seem afraid at all.

Orion still had his fist raised, but he took a step forward, bringing the rat farther into the circle of light from his sword. I let out a gasp as three more pairs of eyes glinted at the edge of the dark. More rats sat behind the first, watching us with the same clinical gaze.

Suddenly I found myself wondering what the Pied Piper in the fable did with all the rats she led away from the village. For some reason, I now had a sneaking suspicion she'd kept them. Orion thrust his sword higher, and as the light spread, I let out a shriek of terror.

The room that the tunnel opened up into was a cylinder. It rose up above us, and there were more tunnels in the walls around us. But the layout of the chamber wasn't what scared me. A sea of glittering black eyes stared at us from all sides. There were rats on the floor with us. There were rats on the walls around us. There were rats on the *ceiling* above us.

And in the corner, an unnaturally bright dandelion grew in the muck.

For a moment the world was still. I couldn't hear anything, but that was thanks to the three layers of noise-canceling devices I was wearing. Then as one, the army of rats began to scamper forward, and all hell broke loose.

I **WAS SCREAMING.**

I couldn't hear it, but I could *feel* it. My chest burned with the need for air, and my jaw ached from being held open. The assault rifle in my hands bucked as I sprayed the sea of rats with lead. Alex's rifle blazed away next to mine, and the flashes of our muzzles illuminated the room in strobing bursts of light like it was a low-budget action movie.

There was no time to aim. But then, there was no need to either. I couldn't miss them if I wanted to. The furry horde charged us, flowing like an ocean wave, and everywhere my weapon tracked, the leading edge of the flood was beaten back. The rounds in my gun were made of cold forged iron, a special process that made them more dangerous to supernatural creatures. They were designed for combat, to penetrate body armor and bring down things the size of human beings. Against rats, they were beyond overkill. It was like using a full-sized crane and wrecking ball to take apart a Lego house.

Vermin exploded in bursts of red viscera, but still they came, driven by the devilish song of the Pied Piper, daughter of the Siren. Abruptly my weapon jerked to a halt in my hands as I emptied the magazine. Cursing, I ejected the mag and grabbed another from my belt.

Without my fire to keep the horde at bay, they closed the distance. Visions of the army of rodents flowing over me, biting, biting, biting until they tore me into tiny shreds, played in my mind. The Hunter flowed into the space left by my reloading, and his fiery blade swept in a low arc. A dozen rodents vanished, felled like stalks of wheat by a reaper. My new magazine locked into place, and I pulled the slide back.

"Clear!" I shouted, grateful that he could still hear. The Hunter leapt backward, and I opened fire once more, beating back at the furry wave. Orion dashed past me, going to spell Alex.

Despair filled me as I glanced at the furry ocean swirling around us. Even if I managed to hit more than one rat with every bullet, I knew I wouldn't have enough. We were outnumbered a billion to three. The tide might be held back for a moment, but it was obvious how the battle was going to end.

This had been a trap. The Piper had been ready for us to follow her into the seat of her power, and we were woefully unprepared. A great sadness bloomed in my chest as I realized that I was likely going to die in this sewer, eaten alive by rats. My soul would go to Hell, my friends' lives would be ruined, and my sister would be left to fend for herself.

What a failure.

A dozen rats dropped from the ceiling, landing on and around me like rodent paratroopers. I screamed, releasing the grip on my rifle so I could swat at the creatures on me. I could feel their claws scrabbling for purchase on the thick cloth of my fatigues. I spun, knocking several of the rats free. They danced around my legs, and I stomped at them with my boots. I felt one on my shoulder and punched it off me without looking.

Freed from my attackers, I grabbed my rifle to resume firing, driving back the encroaching wave. Now that they were closer, I could see that every time I fired, the entire horde flinched.

It was the noise, I realized. Just as the gunshots that Orion had fired when the Piper put me under her thrall had broken me out, ours were conflicting with her control now. But for some reason, it wasn't enough to break her hold. Maybe it's because rats are stupider than humans, or maybe she had given them a stronger dose of the song since she had time to prepare.

After a moment of thought, I flicked the lever on the side of my rifle to toggle it from semi-automatic to fully automatic. I braced myself against the gun and squeezed the trigger.

The downsides of firing a fully automatic rifle mostly have to do with loss of precision. Once you're spraying lead, it can be hard to keep the recoil of the weapon under control, and it's dangerous to just let bullets fly willy-nilly. Fortunately for me, I was basically aiming at the ocean.

As I lit into the rats, I watched the ones I wasn't shooting to see if my plan was making a difference. In each burst of light, I saw the interruption flow through the group like an aftershock, starting with the ones closest to me and rippling onward.

With every gunshot, a new wave began, and they came so quickly that the whole army was vibrating. I swept my gun back and forth, and a grin grew on my face as the front line of rodents disintegrated—not from my bullets, but from the sound.

The leading charge broke, and it was like a dam collapsing. The horde shattered, and rats scattered, fleeing into the tunnels and the dark to get away from the light and sound of the humans. In seconds, they were gone.

Slowly, I lowered my weapon. My hands were shaking, and it was only thanks to the relentless drills Orion had put us through that I was able to reload my weapon. The three of us stood in the warm light of the Hunter's sword, and I gazed around the room in horror.

It was a war zone. The muddy floor had been torn to shreds by our weapons. Blood and guts were everywhere. As the acrid stench of gunpowder began to fade, the rotten scent of death began to permeate everything. I closed my eyes and looked away, not sure I could stomach another second.

A hand tapped me on the shoulder, and I turned to face Alex. His face was paler than usual, and his eyes were wide. He gave me a nervous smile and tapped his own ear protection. He was making sure I was okay. I wasn't. But I hadn't been bitten, and that was good news. I gave him a thumbs-up, and he copied it.

Orion gave us both an impatient wave and gestured toward one of the tunnels leading farther into the dark. The Hunter had his prey in his sights, and he would not tarry any longer. That was fine with me, I had no desire to stay in this room for even another second. Gingerly, I made my way through the rat graveyard to the other side. We resumed our triangular formation, and Orion led us onward.

The empty vacuum of white noise pumping through my headphones was almost strangling me. My breathing was ragged, and it echoed in my head loudly enough to overcome my protection. Annoyed, I dug out my phone and changed the playlist from white noise to music. Elegant piano began, dampened slightly by the plugs in my ear canals. It sounded like the stuff they would play in the elevator of a fancy dentist's office. Whatever it was, it helped drown out my panting, and that was good enough.

We made our way deeper into the network of tunnels, pausing every so often so Orion could check the ground for the tracks of his prey. For my part, I glared into the outer darkness, sweeping my rifle back and forth, looking for the beady eyes of rats.

Our path remained rodent-free, and as we took turn after turn, I began to despair that I would ever see the sun again. We had only been underground for about an hour, but already it was beginning to feel like an eternity.

Then in the distance, we saw it. A single light, like the North Star, guiding us home. I gestured at it but needn't have bothered. The Hunter had better eyes than an eagle and had seen it long before I did.

My hands began to shake as my heart rate skyrocketed once more. This had to be the Piper's lair. As we drew nearer, I saw the light was coming from a room that our tunnel emerged into. Orion sheathed his sword, and Alex and I turned off our flashlights. Together we crept up to the edge of the darkness and peered down on the workshop below.

Clarissa had been planning this for a long time. She had taken over another cylinder intersection, although this was much bigger than the last. Giant pillars ringed the room. As deep as we were, the floor was another dozen feet below us. The entire place burned with shop lights, and I had to squint as my eyes adjusted to the searing brightness. In the far corner, I saw a generator and what I thought were dehumidifiers, helping to keep this place livable.

Several armed guards stood watch around the perimeter of the space, dressed in the same black fatigues that Clarissa had worn. They stood with the rigid, uniform precision of Beefeaters keeping watch before Buckingham Palace.

In the middle of the room, a series of long tables had been set out. On the center were the remains of something horrible. I know the Siren had appeared to Odysseus and his companions as a beautiful woman, but the corpse she left behind was most definitely not.

The body was long, too long. I'd guess it stretched over twelve feet. Desiccated, scaly flesh clung to the bones. There was something immediately *monstrous* about their form that I could not explain. A sinister evil that radiated from them like a smell.

Harmony, our missing Nephilim, stood at the table next to Peisinoe's remains, working with some power tools. I felt a burst of relief at the sight of her laboring away. We weren't too late; the new bone flute was still being made. But also, Harmony was alive! We still had time to save her. At the center of it all, like a queen ant lurking in her warren, was Clarissa, the Pied Piper herself. She stood at the head of her mother's remains, staring down at them with a feverish intensity.

I glanced at Orion, waiting for instructions. The Hunter perched at the edge of the tunnel, brooding. Finally, he nodded once and looked at me. Holding his hand sideways, he pointed to the right edge of the room. Turning to Alex, he repeated the gesture, sending him to the left.

I arched an eyebrow and pointed at him, asking where he would be going. He pointed at the center of the room, right at Clarissa.

I don't know why I'd bothered asking. Where else would he go but right after the monster?

I shrugged and nodded. He gave me a tight grin, the one that only comes out when he's fighting. His black eyes danced with a dark light. He is the Hunter. This is what he lives for. That's why they gave him the Constellation. Without so much as a countdown, Orion drew his sword and leapt out of the tunnel, landing in a crouch.

"Clarissa!" he bellowed, standing tall with his blade burning in his right hand. Well, I assume that's what he said. My lip-reading isn't great. I was so shocked that for a moment, I forgot his instructions and could only gape in awe as he declared himself. He may not be subtle, but he certainly has a flair for the dramatic. Then, shaking myself, I followed my orders, dropping down behind him and making my way around the right side of the ring until I could duck behind one of the pillars. Slowly, I sighted my rifle in on one of the armed guards and waited.

The Piper's head snapped up, and she turned her gaze from the remains of the Siren to the man who'd killed her. Her mouth opened in a vicious snarl, and it stretched too open and too wide, revealing row upon row of pointed teeth.

"I come in shopping"—no, that can't be right—"judgment!" read the Hunter's lips, and then he charged.

The guards around the ring chose that moment to act. As one, just like the rats that had attacked us in the tunnels, they turned, raising their weapons and opening fire. Orion zigged to the side, and I watched as the ground exploded, torn to shreds by bullets.

With a heavy heart, I watched the guards. They moved like marionette puppets, as if another presence controlled their every move and was bad at it. I guess the Pied Piper had kept the kids along with the rats and turned them all into her slaves. These couldn't be the ones from the original fables; that was centuries ago. Maybe they were descendants of the originals or just their replacements, raised from birth to be fully devoted drones. Disgust built in me. At least the Siren had just killed and eaten the sailors she beguiled. This somehow felt even more warped and twisted.

In some ways, killing them would be a mercy. In others it was yet another horror that the world forced upon me. The cruel math was simple: Either I shot them, or they shot my friend. It's selfish and ugly, but I'd make the same decision every time.

But just because I had to shoot this guard didn't mean I had to kill him. I dropped my aim to the man's leg and squeezed off a round. I'm not a bad shot, and this was about as easy as it gets. Hitting a stationary target a couple dozen feet away is like shooting the broadside of a barn for anyone with a little practice. That's what makes these things so dangerous.

The bullet slammed into the man, but he barely reacted. His body twitched, responding to the physical force of the round as it hit him, but his face didn't change. He didn't fall or even look my way. Instead, he kept firing at Orion, tracking him with his jerky movements.

A well of sorrow burst open in my heart as I realized that Clarissa's control of these stolen souls was so absolute, there was no freeing them. I couldn't just incapacitate them and deal with them later. I had to save Orion now.

The cheerful piano music that my phone was piping into my headphones trilled along, oblivious to the death that I was about to participate in.

Swallowing the rising bile in my throat, I raised my sights to center mass and fired two quick rounds. The guard spun, hammered by my shots, and this time he fell. Turning off my brain so I couldn't think about it anymore, I spun to the next guard and shot him. Judging by the still forms lying around the room, I could tell that Alex was doing the same on his side of the ring.

I felt a small amount of relief to see that he had chosen to shoot the thralls too. It's selfish and terrible, but if he had come up with a way to save them, my guilt would only have been compounded.

I was so distracted by my moral quandary that I missed one. The guard had been behind us, and when we jumped out of the tunnel, no one had noticed him lurking at our rear. The thrall tackled me, his jerky movements not gentle in any way. We went down in a pile of limbs, and my gun went flying. So did my bulky noise-canceling headphones, leaving me with only two layers of sonic defense.

I must have landed on my phone, because the piano music blasting in my ears abruptly vanished, only to be replaced by intense Gregorian chanting. What had happened to me that I had transformed from a normal boy into someone fighting the thralls of the Pied Piper with cinematic accompaniment?

No time for existential panic; that was for when I was trying to fall asleep. This was the time to focus on not getting stabbed. I brought my knee up hard, driving it into the guard's stomach. Just like the one I had shot, he didn't react. Whatever Clarissa had done to him had numbed him beyond the point of pain.

Iron hands clamped down on one of my arms, trying to wrestle me to the ground. Raising my left elbow, I drove it down on his wrist, but it bounced off as if he were made of steel. I couldn't break his grip.

I rolled to the side, twisting so my left hand could reach down to my thigh, where a combat knife was strapped. The guard followed me with heedless aggression, trying to pin me. I flailed with my non-dominant hand to undo the snaps and free the blade, but I was too slow, not ambidextrous enough to save my own life.

The guard rolled on top of me, trapping my other arm against the ground with his knees, and I could only watch in terror as he drew back his free hand in a fist aimed right at my neck. Before the strike could land, a hail of bullets slammed into him, knocking him off me like a minor hurricane.

Gasping for breath, I scrambled to my feet and grabbed my fallen rifle. I trained it on my attacker, but he didn't so much as twitch. I don't care how magical the music filling his ears canals was, it couldn't plug the holes the bullets had left.

I glanced up to see Alex give me a grim salute from across the room. I nodded at him, and we both turned back to our work. While we were taking out the guards, Orion had closed with Clarissa. I watched in mild awe as my mentor lunged toward her, blazing blade extended.

The Pied Piper had continued to shift her form as the Hunter charged. She was taller now; her legs had apparently fused together to form a massive snake-like tail. I don't know how someone can shapeshift and increase in total mass—that feels like something physics would say is impossible. But who was I to disbelieve what I was seeing with my own eyes?

Hissing with rage, she danced backward from his attack, incredibly swift on her scaly appendage. Clarissa swiped at Orion once with a clawed hand before spinning and slithering toward where Harmony worked away. The blond Nephilim hadn't reacted in the slightest to the battle raging around her. Her eyes remained focused on the task in front of her, trapped in some world of the Piper's devising.

"Dun Dun, Dun dun!!" the chorus chanting in my head sang ominously. We were in big trouble.

Clarissa snatched up something from the workshop table and wielded it in front of her like a scepter. It was made of bone, like her original pipe, but larger, suited to her massive monster frame. If her last instrument had been a flute, this was a trumpet. Harmony didn't even seem to notice it was gone; she just kept working on a smaller piece in front of her, like a diligent ant.

We may have interrupted the Nephilim before she was done, but not before Clarissa had gotten something new to use. I don't know that much about music or instruments, but from my casual observation, the bigger they are, the *deeper* the sound they tend to make. That's probably an oversimplification that would make any composer roll their eyes, but in this case, it seemed true enough.

A deep bass note emerged from the trumpet. It was so low that I could feel it vibrating in my chest like a miniature earthquake. No headphones could protect me from the wall of sound that came from the Siren's bone instrument. It rang like the call of some ancient beast waking in the deep, like the voice of some long-dead god. I felt its chill in my bones.

Clenching my teeth and bracing myself, I tried to fortify my mind against the Piper's new weapon. But my world did not fade; I was not pursued by new nightmares. Instead I remained in the waking world to witness a real horror.

Orion staggered under the sonic force. I could only imagine how overwhelming it must have been hearing it so close and not wearing any earplugs. But the Hunter did not waver for more than a second, and as the ungodly note faded, he resumed his charge toward Clarissa.

In the shadows of the tunnel behind the half Siren, something stirred. It took me a moment to process its sheer size as it scuttled out of the ink. It was covered in matte-black chitin so dark that it was swallowed by the blackness of the tunnels.

The clicking of its feet on the cement was loud enough to hear over the soundtrack blasting in my ears. Each step sent terrifying shivers down my spine. It seemed that Clarissa's new instrument gave her power over more than mice and men. By the time the thing emerged into the light, I was already terrified.

I hate bugs.

And while I think scorpions are technically some sort of arachnid-slash-spider-cousin and not a bug, I don't care. If they have more than four legs and are covered in an exoskeleton, I *hate* them. No exceptions.

What walked out to confront us was a black scorpion bigger than Alex's minivan. Just in case that's not properly conveying the monstrosity we were facing, let me try it another way. This thing—this ancient horror that should have been in its lair underneath one of the pyramids—was over twelve feet long. Its tail curled a good eight feet above its head and was tipped with a vicious barb. If scorpions had a king, this was it.

I don't think an entire can of bug spray would so much as make it cough.

Clarissa slid backward to meet the monster like an owner with a pet. She smiled a horrible smile as she placed a hand on one of its massive pincers. The thing paused at her side, quivering.

The Piper called something to the Hunter, a mocking expression on her face. Seeing no sign of her other flute, I risked prying up the edge of my headphones to hear what she had to say. I could see the tension in Orion's broad shoulders as he stared at the creature. From the set of his jaw, I didn't think he liked scorpions any more than I did.

"Sometimes I think I should be grateful for you, Hunter!" Clarissa's voice was cruel. "You killed my mother and made me an orphan, but you freed me. Once she was dead, the gods didn't care if I left the island. My mother never understood the depths of her *power*—but now, thanks to you, I can finally realize it in her name! Even the gods will tremble." She raised the trumpet to her lips again. I released my grip on the headphones, letting them snap back into place over my ears. They slammed shut just in time for her to let out another deep bass note.

The scorpion at her side lunged forward like a junkyard dog let off the leash. It barreled toward Orion, and the Hunter raised his sword, ready to meet it in the center of the arena.

"Dun dun!" sang the music in my ears.

BLACK LIGHTNING FLASHED as the scorpion's tail shot forward like a spear, search-ing for the Hunter. Orion rolled to the side, flaming blade rising in a neat parry. The monster curled its tail back, letting it hover above its body like Death's scythe. Unlike Clarissa's other thralls, who had been jerky and clumsy in their movements, this monster was fluid like a black river. Another benefit of Harmony's craftsmanship, no doubt.

Sparks flared on the side of the beast as Alex began shoot-ing from across the arena. Kicking myself for wasting time, I opened fire on the monster. While a normal, run-of-the-mill North American scorpion would stand no chance against the

5.56 mm rounds that Alex and I were carrying, the chitin on this fell thing was made of sterner stuff.

I traced my rounds along the side of its armored carapace, looking for a weak spot. But all I saw were sparks as my bullets bounced off harmlessly. It lunged toward Orion, and I held my fire, not wanting to risk hitting my friend with a ricochet.

Orion shook off his own fear and danced forward, gliding on light feet to meet the scorpion king. His fiery sword blazed as he danced around the beast's pincer, which was darting at him. The Hunter spun, letting his momentum carry him backward along the scorpion's side. As he completed his turn, he flicked the blade out, shearing through one of the minor legs with ease.

Dark ichor spewed from the wound as the two of them passed each other. Orion spun again and sprinted after it, trying to stay behind its tail. It was truly incredible to witness. Sword fighting is an art, and while it's easy to focus on the big strokes as the hard part, they really aren't.

The artistry is in the footwork. The greatest swordsmen are ballet dancers who missed their true calling and have a little extra trauma. Studying underneath the big guy for four months gave me just a glimmer of how much I did not know. His easy pirouettes around the scorpion were something I could only dream of.

Orion tried to stab into the scorpion's blind spot, but arachnids scuttle *fast*. The black armored beast twisted with lightning speed, its claws shooting out to grab the Hunter. Without time to retreat, the Hunter leapt over them. His mouth opened as he screamed in rage, sword blazing over his head, ready to deliver a devastating blow to the creature's midsection.

Before he could land it, the scorpion's tail batted him out of the air like a Nephilim swatter. The vicious appendage whipped forward, catching our boss in the side and knocking him off course. He landed on the floor of our mucky arena in a pile, his flaming blade tumbling out of his grip.

I forgot how to breathe.

I've seen Orion fight Immortals, some truly apex predators of the universe, but I'd never seen him take a hit like that. For a moment, the arena was still. The king looked down at the limp form of Orion like a dog waiting to see if its opponent would get up.

Then, after a second, it took a step toward him.

As one, Alex and I raised our rifles and opened fire on the beast. I knew we probably couldn't hurt the thing, but we might distract it long enough for Orion to get back to his feet. Standing off to the side of the scorpion, I tracked my aim along the center of its mass before settling in on the peaked ridge at the front of its carapace, where the black orbs the size of baseballs that it used for eyes were.

I bet those weren't armored.

Exhaling a long breath, I let the rifle in my hands settle, as I had been taught. Before, I had been shooting recklessly, just trying to overwhelm the thing's armor with firepower. But now I had a target, and I was a student of the Hunter.

The first lesson was how to hit your target.

My finger squeezed the trigger, and I rode the recoil of the weapon, keeping my aim on the beast. Sparks flew from the base of its carapace, just a few inches too low. It took another step toward the downed form of Orion. I raised my weapon a hair and squeezed again.

The reaction was immediate. The scorpion spun in a circle,

mad with agony. After doing a full revolution, it exploded out of its swirl toward me like it was its own bullet. I didn't even have time to blink before it was on me.

Desperate, I threw myself to the side, narrowly avoiding the barb of its tail that sailed through the spot where my face had just been.

"Dun dun!" Why was that on loop?

I landed in a roll, coming through it to my feet and breaking into a terrified sprint. I could feel the thing chasing me, but I didn't dare look. I dashed to one of the support beams on the edge of the ring and jumped behind it, using it as a shield between me and the beast.

The scorpion slammed into the other side, blinded by my bullet or by rage. Claws reached around from either side, but I ducked away from them, using every trick I'd learned on the recess playground to keep the monster on the other side.

We danced, my quick thinking and a six-foot-diameter pillar the only reason that I didn't die instantly. The scorpion was a true monster, but it wasn't smart. Well, it wasn't as smart as I am, anyway.

Unfortunately, its master knew that I was merely a distraction. After a few moments, the dull, throbbing note from Clarissa's trumpet sounded again, and the scorpion turned away, heading back toward the center of the arena. The Piper must have grown tired of my games.

Cautiously, I peeked around the pillar, watching the monster as it stalked back toward the Hunter. My gambit had worked—Orion was back on his feet! Hope surged in me as our champion rose to face the scorpion. There was a grimace on his face, as if he was still shaking off the hit, but otherwise he looked okay.

Suddenly his leather jacket began to smoke. In one fluid motion, he ripped it off himself and threw it to the ground. There it continued to steam, being eaten by whatever acid was in the monster's tail. His shirt showed no signs of burning. The stinger must have gotten caught in his jacket and been unable to penetrate to his skin underneath.

We were back.

Wincing in pain, Orion picked up his sword and extended it toward the scorpion in a flourish, inviting it to charge him. I don't think the arachnid understood him, but its standing orders were to attack, and it was more than happy to.

The monster surged toward the Hunter, and they met in a clash of black armor and fire. I raised my rifle, hoping to pick off the beast's other eye. But as I sighted in on it, I was shown the downfall of having no hearing on the battlefield—it makes you very easy to sneak up on.

I caught a blur of motion out of the corner of my eye just before something hit me with the force of a small train. Then I was flying, spinning end-over-end. My landing was not graceful in the slightest, and I skidded a few feet through the wet muck before finally coming to a halt.

"Foul ball!" I gasped, trying to sit up to face the Pied Piper.

Clarissa slithered toward me on her grotesque tail. Still rattled, I raised my rifle and opened fire. She might have a few scales, but I didn't think she was as bulletproof as her pet. My first round went wide. I centered myself and fired again. The shapeshifter rocked back as my bullet slammed into her chest. Then my rifle clicked on empty.

Crap.

Without time to reload, I leapt to my feet and tried to

hobble out of the way of her charge. But unlike her beast, she was at least as smart as I am, and she surged to the side, cutting me off from the pillars.

Her long, bony arms reached for me, fingers tipped with horrible claws. The giant mouth that was full of shark teeth opened wide, eager to feast on me. I wondered if this was the last thing that sailors who survived crashing into her mother's rocks had seen before they were devoured.

Hell, here I come.

Bullets hammered into her side as Alex noticed my plight and came to my aid. The shapeshifter's gaze snapped to my friend across the arena, buying me a few precious seconds.

Numb with terror, my body fell into practiced rhythms. The reason people lock up when they're afraid is because they can't form new thoughts. Fear makes your mind go blank. But your body doesn't really need you to think about most of the things it does.

Fortunately for me, Orion had forced me to practice reloading so many times that it felt like the most natural thing for me to be doing. My lungs breathed, my heart beat, my hands reloaded. There were no differences among these involuntary things, and my fingers flew through the motions without any input from me.

My empty magazine bounced at my feet. The fresh one—my last—snapped into place. I pulled the slide, chambering the first round. The weapon rose almost of its own accord, and I placed my cheek on the stock, sighting down its barrel. Clarissa, warned by some sound or motion, turned from Alex to me and found herself staring down the bore of my assault rifle.

My finger flipped the lever from semi-automatic to full.

Her eyes widened.

I squeezed the trigger, unleashing a torrent of cold iron rounds into her. She slithered to the side, trying to dodge, but it was too late. We were too close; there was nowhere for her to go. The Piper was knocked end-over-tail by the force of my rounds as they slammed into her chest with the fury of a thousand killer bees.

I don't care how immortal your parents were, that had to *hurt.*

My finger stayed tight on the trigger, pinning the shape-shifter to the ground with a hailstorm of lead. I didn't think it would kill her. She'd proved resistant to bullets before. It would take something with a little more oomph behind it to kill her once and for all, and our only supercharged weapon was currently busy. But the steam pouring out of her chest where the cold iron burned her gave me a little hope.

I felt rather than heard my rifle click on empty. Panting with exertion, I glared down at the writing form of the Pied Piper. She was definitely still alive but in excruciating pain.

Alex ran up beside me and without a moment's hesitation emptied his clip into Clarissa. Her giant mouth opened in a scream that I could dimly hear over the sound of the chanters on loop. Her tortured voice sent a shudder down my spine as her primal cry penetrated my noise bubble. Alex and I exchanged long glances.

"This is a terrible boss fight!" I said. He shrugged, still unable to hear me.

Turning my back on the wounded Piper, I look for Orion, terrified of what I might find. But I needn't have worried. The Hunter was still alive and locked in his duel with the king scorpion. The arachnid seemed to be confused. It staggered drunkenly to the side as it raced at Orion. The big Nephilim danced with it, forcing it to circle him as they closed. Even to my mortal eyes, the scorpion seemed slower than it had before. Had Orion tired it out, or was something else at play?

Curious, I glanced at the center of the room where Harmony had been working. The blond woman was sitting at her table with her head in her hands. As I watched, she looked around the room with a dazed sense of horror.

An idea began to form in my mind, and I turned back to check on Clarissa's status. The Pied Piper was still on the ground, writhing in pain. I knew that the cold iron would eventually work its way through her body, and then she could begin healing. But it seemed like until she was back on her feet, her ability to control others was interrupted.

My gaze snapped around the room, looking for the trumpet she had dropped. If I could break it while she was down, I could stop her from ever pipering again. I spotted the bone instrument twenty feet away, well in the scorpion's range. So much for that. Time for Plan B.

This was our chance. Orion chose his moment and stepped toward the scorpion. The Hunter's fiery blade licked out to deflect one of the massive claws as it tried to grab him. Then he stepped back as the other pincer swept through where he had just been standing, his face unbothered. Once again, the scorpion's tail shot forward, hurtling like a spear for his chest.

Orion turned sideways, letting the barb shoot past him harmlessly. His sword rose and fell in one vicious stroke, striking the chitinous tail right behind the bulb that held the stinger. The fiery blade sliced cleanly through the joint, and the bulb fell to the ground in another spray of black blood. The scorpion retreated, disarmed—or was it distailed? Never one for mercy, the Hunter pressed his advantage. He chased the fleeing monster, battering it with his blade. Each stroke left a smoking scratch on its armor as Orion vented his fury on the creature. Its death was only a matter of time.

I was out of ammo for my rifle, so I decided to make myself useful by checking on the victim. I waved at Alex for him to follow me, and together we made our way around the outside edge of the circle to where Harmony was sitting. She was bowed over the table, with her head in her hands, and her shoulders shook with sobs.

The desiccated flesh and bones of Peisinoe the Siren lay on the table before her, along with what looked like the Piper's original flute. I felt my mouth twist in disgust looking at the ancient and terrible remains laid out like arts and crafts supplies. Orion should have thrown her whole corpse into the volcano for good measure.

Glancing once more at the twisting figure of the Pied Piper, I decided to risk it and pulled my headphones off my ears, freeing me from the incessant loop of music. Even if I did end up getting my mind clobbered by her musical powers, I didn't know how much more of that I could take.

"Hey, are you okay?" I called, reaching out a hand for her shoulder. She flailed in panic at my touch, spinning in her seat and swatting my wrist with impressive strength.

"Whoa, whoa!" I shouted, taking a step back and holding up my hands to show her I meant no harm. "I'm one of the good guys. We're here to rescue you. You're Harmony, right? We were at your house?"

The Nephilim's eyes cleared a little at my words, and she blinked slowly. She looked like she had just woken up from a generational nap and had no idea where she was. I could relate. Even the light version of Clarissa's music had left me dazed and confused. I'm sure a full dose would hit like a ton of bricks.

"She made me do it," Harmony cried as her memories returned. She dropped her head in her hands and sobbed once more.

"I know," I said as comfortingly as I could. "We saw the trumpet. But you had no choice. She was controlling you."

"I swore an oath!" she screamed, weeping hysterically now. "I made a solemn vow, and I have *broken* it."

"What kind of oath?" I asked, exchanging a concerned look with Alex. He still had his headgear on, but our body language wasn't exactly subtle. He didn't need to be able to hear our conversation to see it wasn't going well.

"To make no weapons. To only use my arts for beauty and not for war."

"Well, it was kind of beautiful, if you think about it," I offered, glancing over to where the trumpet lay on the ground. "It might not count."

"You don't understand," she sobbed, not looking at me. "She will kill me."

"Who?" I asked, still not following.

CRACK.

My interrogation was interrupted by the horrible crunch of something shattering. I spun in time to see Orion standing on the top of the monster, pulling his blade out of its head. He rode it down with the casual balance of a surfboarder.

The great beast's legs gave out, and it collapsed to the floor.

The tension bled out of its tail, and it seemed to deflate, shrinking in on itself as its life faded. It gave one final rattle as the Hunter stepped off its carcass with a grim smile on his face. His gray shirt was sliced in two places, but he seemed otherwise fine.

He strode toward us, burning blade still gripped firmly in his hand. Harmony let out a little squeak, maybe in fear or maybe from something more like fangirling. Orion has that effect on a lot of the junior Nephilim. But honestly, who could blame them?

"Are you hurt?" he asked Harmony, dropping into a crouch in front of her. His brow was furrowed in eager concentration. The yoke of responsibility that he wore on his shoulders as the owner of this territory demanded that he protect his tribe.

"Not physically," she sobbed, collapsing back into her hands. "But I have broken an oath to my great-great-great-grandmother."

"Mese?" I asked, and she nodded.

"She made me swear not to use her heritage for violence, only beauty, and I have broken that. Mese, Mese, Mese, hear my words and accept my apology." I blinked in surprise at her begging the empty air. It seemed a little premature to start asking for—

"Yes, child, you have." A woman's voice, full of power and chimes, rang out behind us.

All the air seemed to be sucked out of the room. As one, we whirled to face the stranger standing in the center. She was tall, taller than Orion. It was hard to gauge in that underground ring, but I'd have guessed she towered to at least ten feet.

She wore a thick white veil that cascaded down over her face, obscuring her completely. She was dressed in a matching pale dress and gladiator sandals whose straps wrapped around her ankles like serpents. My jaw dropped as I realized that Harmony had just summoned her ancestor into a circle that we were all inside. That is not how you're supposed to do it. There's no protection from Immortals when you're both on the same side of the line.

"You have broken your vow, and you must pay the price," announced Mese, the middle note of the Muses, looming over us like a specter of judgment.

FORGIVE ME!" HARMONY begged once more, dropping to her knees in front of her demigod ancestor. Tears flowed freely down her face as she groveled. I felt a surge of pity. This poor girl had been caught up in something much bigger than herself. She hadn't made the choice to break her oath; it had been made for her, under coercion. I know how terrible that feels.

"I asked one thing of you, *Harmony*," Mese replied furiously, staring down at her descendant. The chimes in her voice rang with the force of a hurricane. "One rule for the power that you carry in your bloodline, and you couldn't even follow through with that, could you?"

"It wasn't her fault!" I shouted, stepping forward to face the Muse. I didn't mean to. But Harmony had been through enough. She deserved to have someone stick up for her against the…ancient Immortal being. The giant woman twitched, and the veiled face turned toward us as if seeing us for the first time.

"You dare interrupt your betters, mortal?" she intoned. Mese took an aggressive step in my direction, which proved to be a mistake.

In the flash of an eye, Orion was between us. I swear I didn't even see him move. One moment the giantess was bearing down on me, the next the Hunter barred her way. His flaming sword hung loosely in his right hand, pointing at the ground. It was a non-threatening gesture, if such a thing is possible for him. Not a challenge, merely a warning.

Mese froze in the way of immortals. Every fiber of her being seemed to lock in place for a moment as shock knocked her outside of Time itself. "You," she breathed slowly. "Why am I not surprised to find you at the center of destroying my family once more?"

"He's rescuing her, actually," I sneered, hovering behind my boss like one of those yappy little schnauzers barking at a rottweiler. "She was kidnapped!"

"SILENCE," Mese roared. But all was not silent.

A dark, horrible note sounded from the deep. The world seemed to slow down as the fell note played. I felt sluggish, as if giant pressure was holding me down under its crushing weight. Suddenly I missed my chanting soundtrack.

Slowly, I twisted my neck, looking back to where Clarissa had been lying in the muck. The serpent-like Piper had managed to get back on her…tail. She was holding the bone trumpet that Harmony had fashioned to her terrifying lips and playing her dreadful note.

I felt the weight of this fell trumpet's music as it passed me by. Like the song for the scorpion, it wasn't meant for me. The Muse staggered backward several paces as the dark song filled her ears. She let out a groan of anguish that echoed with discordant bells.

Suddenly I wondered if Harmony had only been a piece of the puzzle. Clarissa had come to LA to collect people with certain abilities to make her a more powerful weapon. But Harmony was only the grandchild of Mese, a cousin to the daughter of a Siren. Clarissa was a pale shadow of her mother. What was the difference between a descendant and an original Muse? I knew they were responsible for inspiration, especially when it related to music… A terrifying thought wormed its way into my mind as I listened to that dreadful song. I had already experienced firsthand the shortcomings of the Piper's music. It could coerce, but it wasn't perfect.

Music has at least three parts to it: the skill of the performer playing the piece, the quality of the instrument that makes the notes, and the talent of the composer who wrote it. An out-of-tune instrument could ruin a performance, but the best violin in the world couldn't turn something I wrote into a concert that rivaled one of Mozart's. Could Clarissa force the Muse to help her compose songs of control that could not be broken? With the perfect tools, could she use her mother's bones to enslave the very gods she was seeking vengeance against?

The shapeshifter paused, taking a deep breath before resuming the long note. Mese staggered again, holding both of her hands to her head, trying to ward off the melodic attack. But the sonic waves were like a besieging army, and eventually they overcame her mind's walls. Only when Mese stopped struggling did Clarissa release the note and let the trumpet fall from her hands to the ground below. A cruel smile spread across her face, and she clapped with delight.

"Oh, Harmony, you outdid yourself," she cooed into the sudden silence. "You have given me golden chains to cage Zeus himself. My dear, with your talents, I shall rule this world." I felt a flicker of fear. I had guessed part of her plan, but the whole *world?* That was a bigger scope than I had anticipated. Suddenly the chains encircling the world in Sibyl's final warning seemed a lot less metaphorical than they original had.

Harmony let out a low moan of despair.

"Mese, darling, we have so much work to do. But first—" Clarissa's eyes narrowed with vicious delight. "—be a good demigod and kill the Hunter and his pups for me?" I swallowed as the giant woman's shrouded gaze turned to us in robotic movements.

Then the Muse exploded forward with violent power and struck at Orion. She was so fast that she made the king scorpion seem like a decrepit retiree. It was only as she moved that I remembered that her father was supposedly Apollo. What did that mean? I don't really know. No one has bothered to explain it to the new guy.

I knew that Orion was a Nephilim, a descendant of a demon and a human. I knew that Apollo and all the other beings are real, but that doesn't always mean that people are who they say they are. What it does mean is that they have the power to back up the title of "god" without anyone questioning it.

But as fast as this demigod was, the Hunter was something else entirely.

Mese blurred through the space where Orion had been standing, but he was gone. He stepped out of range of her strike and flowed around her fists. As I watched, he slowly raised his blade and slid it home into the sheath over his shoulder.

I'd seen him do this once before, when he fought someone he did not want to kill. A chill ran down my spine as I realized the implications of that. There are only a few reasons that the Hunter would choose *not* to finish an enemy.

Orion can be a little…straightforward when it comes to solving problems. He has no problem executing things that get in his way. The only reason that he wouldn't want to cut down Mese is because he knew he wasn't supposed to. Killing a daughter of Apollo would have *repercussions*, and he was trying to avoid those. Which meant we were going to have to find a different way out of this problem.

"This is so bad," Alex shouted to me, ripping off his own headphones. We both still had the plugs in our ear canals, but they only dampened my hearing; Alex sounded as if he were yelling at me underwater.

"We gotta figure out how to break her free!" I yelled back, waving at our boss, who was ducking and weaving backward through the ring. "He doesn't want to kill her."

"He put the sword away!" Alex gestured wildly at Orion. "Do you know what that means?" Okay, maybe these earplugs were a little better at their jobs than I thought.

"Watch out!" Harmony screamed. I snapped my head in her direction just in time to see Clarissa diving at us like a hungry anaconda. I shoved Alex out of the way and leapt backward, letting her pass between us like a scaly bus.

Instinctively, I knew what she was coming for. As pissed as

she might be at us, we weren't the prize. My hand shot out, and I scooped up her original bone flute from Harmony's workshop, tucking it into my belt. It was probably a bad idea for her to get her terrifying claws on that right now. The trumpet seemed to be a tool for controlling bigger things; maybe she needed the flute to play the chords that could affect the rest of us.

"Come on!" I shouted, drawing my pistol and breaking into a sprint. My mind raced along with my feet. I didn't think we had a prayer of actually stopping her with the firepower we had left. Maybe with more magazines of cold iron bullets, we'd have a chance of killing her. But the few I had in my handgun would just be enough to make her even madder.

The only upside was that the longer she spent chasing us, the more time Orion had to deal with Mese without having to fight the Piper and the Muse at the same time. I could be a distraction. Being loud and obnoxious was a specialty of mine.

Gripping my weapon tightly, I spun and fired two shots at the shapeshifter. I needn't have bothered. Her eyes were firmly fixed on the flute in my belt. She hissed and gave chase, and we fled deeper into the arena. Alex and I sprinted through the back, where her guards had set up the infrastructure to turn this tunnel into a workshop.

A pair of generators hummed as they fed power to the lights. Inspiration flared in my mind like a match as we raced past them, and I slapped Alex on the shoulder, pointing at them.

"I have an idea!" I shouted.

"Is it what I think it is?" he said with a groan.

"Probably."

"Why is that always your solution to everything?"

"It's worked so far, hasn't it?"

"Not really!"

"Just trust me," I snapped, breaking to the right.

For all his complaints, Alex immediately cut to the left, following my plan. As I suspected, Clarissa wanted her flute back, and she stayed on me, slithering at terrifying speed on her gross tail. I felt a smug smile tug at the corner of my mouth as I ran, splitting up from Alex.

This was horrible and dangerous, but I would be lying if I said it wasn't fun. The Hunt had truly given me a sense of purpose. My life had been empty and lost, but fighting monsters felt…good? Despite everything that had thrust me into this, I was glad to be here.

"Catch!" I called, as the shapeshifter bore down on me. I snatched the flute out of my belt and threw it to Alex like a tomahawk, letting it flip end-over-end. Clarissa's eyes widened in fury as it whirled over her head, and she spun in time to see it land at Alex's feet.

My friend gave her a cheeky grin before scooping it up like a relay baton and breaking into a sprint. This was all part of the plan. Thanks to his Nephilim genetics he's a little faster than I am, with slightly better endurance. It's not a huge difference, but this was a game of inches. I had some trouble to get into while he led the Piper on a wild goose chase for her instrument. Trusting Alex to do what needed to be done, I turned to the generators.

There's an old saying that goes, *Where there's smoke, there's fire.* I think it means something smart about letting people tell you who they are and believing them. But there's also a lesser-known version I like that goes, *Where there's fire, there's fuel.*

Generators need gas to run, which means that Clarissa and her little menagerie would have brought down enough to keep everything lit. I jogged over to the pair of generators and immediately smelled that lovely, eggy scent. A smile spread across my face—I was right. I just had to find it.

I checked the back of the generators and let out a small whoop when I found a pair of the iconic red cans. I grabbed the first only to discover that it was mostly empty, but the other one felt full.

I raced away from the generators and back toward Harmony and the ruins of Peisinoe's corpse, the gas can sloshing in my grip. In the center of the ring, Orion was still dancing around the enchanted Mese. While she was clearly devastatingly strong, she wasn't a fighter—not like the Hunter.

I made it back to Harmony's side and shook her out of her stupor. The younger Nephilim looked up at me with wide eyes as she saw the gasoline in my hands. I gave her a devilish smile. "Hi, it would probably be a good idea for you to move," I informed her.

She scrabbled backward to give me space. I jumped up on the table and looked over my shoulder at where the Piper was still chasing Alex like a hound after a fox. Alex saw me looking, and I gave him a nod letting him know it was time. Abruptly he shifted the angle of his dash, cutting diagonally toward me.

"Hey, Clarissa!" I shouted, giving her a little whistle for good measure. The shapeshifter's terrifying head whipped around, and her eyes went wide with fury as she saw me standing over her mother's corpse. Holding her full attention, I began to pour the gasoline out on the bones and workshop at my feet. "I hope your mom's okay with a Viking funeral," I shouted.

The Piper abandoned her pursuit of Alex and shot at me, slithering across the mucky ground at blithering speed. From the side, Alex sprinted toward me, digging into his pocket for a lighter.

I tracked Clarissa's speed, trying not to let the terror I felt watching the giant monster charge overwhelm me. As she drew near, I twisted the top of the canister, popping it off. Then with the same impish grin, I leapt backward and jerked the canister forward, sending a wall of gas out and right into her eyes.

The Piper slid to a halt and let out a screech of fury and pain. One of her bony, clawed hands came up to scrub at her face, trying to get the fuel out of her eyes. She looked up just in time to see Alex arrive at my side, bronze lighter in hand.

The Pied Piper looked down at the pool of gasoline that she had stopped in, and her gaze snapped back up at us in horror right as he tossed the flame onto the table.

Fire burst to life like a hurricane and swept over the workshop, across Peisinoe's bones, and up Clarissa, climbing her like a tree. The half Siren let out an ungodly screech and dropped to the ground, trying to smother the flames that were eating her.

Unfortunately for her, the ground was also on fire.

Alex and I stood side by side, watching as the inferno devoured her. I guess she was Immortal enough to shrug off a few bullets but not enough to stand up to the hunger of fire. Her death was a horror that I will never fully get out of my mind. The shapeshifter seemed to shrivel as the fire ate the extra mass she had acquired. A horrific burning smell filled the room and remained even after her blackened form was finally still.

Silence, except for the cheery crackling of the fire feasting on the workshop tables, descended on the underground arena. Feeling more than a little sick to my stomach, I turned to check the effect the Piper's demise had on the demigod. Mese had frozen in place, and the Hunter stood a few paces back, watching her warily.

The Muse shook like a wet dog, and her veiled head turned from Orion to the smoking ruins of Clarissa and her mother. My heart raced as I leaned forward trying to make out her expression underneath the lace. Had the Piper's death freed Mese from her control?

At last, she spoke. "I think that someone should explain to me what is happening here," she announced in discordant tones.

"You were bewitched," Orion answered slowly, not relaxing out of his fighting stance.

"By music? Impossible. Nothing could do that but—"

"A Siren?" I guessed, interrupting her. I pointed at the burning remnants of the corpse on the table. "What's the matter, don't recognize Peisinoe when you see her?" The veiled gaze tracked slowly from me to the pyre.

"Her daughter sought to claim Peisinoe's power for her own," Orion continued as if he had not been interrupted. "She used instruments made from her mother's bones to command others."

"I see." There was a world of meaning in those words. The veiled Muse turned to stare at her descendant for a long moment before she looked back at the Hunter. "And my granddaughter?" she asked, the chimes in her voice quieter than they had been before.

"The same thing was done to her," Alex pointed out, gesturing at the nervous Nephilim huddled by the wall of the ring, like a preschooler trying to escape the notice of her parents.

"She was forced to break her oath to you," I agreed.

"And she is under my protection." Orion's voice was as hard

as stone. Harmony's face lit up in wonder at his words. I felt my mouth tug in a tired grin. The floor of this arena already had the body of one Immortal that had tried to stand against Orion; what was one more?

"You never change, do you, Hunter?" I might have been wrong, but I thought Mese sounded amused.

"Not yet," Orion told her.

The Muse was silent for a while, as if mulling over the situation before her. Oaths are serious business to Immortals. The more supercharged someone is, the more inflexible they become. An oath can be binding on a molecular level for someone like Mese.

"It seems to me," she chimed after a long moment of thought, "that my granddaughter was not in her right mind when she broke our compact. It would be ill advised of me to judge her for falling prey to a creature that managed to best even me. Furthermore, all the instruments she made that were in violation of her oath have been cast into the fire. As such, it is as if they have never been."

I felt a rush of relief as I saw Orion relax his stance and stand at ease. It was over.

"Yes," she affirmed after a moment. "That is what I think." The veiled giant turned toward her granddaughter and cocked her head. "Let this be a warning to you, child. The Hunter won't always be there to save you."

"Yes, Grandmother," Harmony gasped through tears of relief. "I will."

With the sound of rushing wind, Mese was gone, leaving the four of us alone in the storm tunnels of Los Angeles.

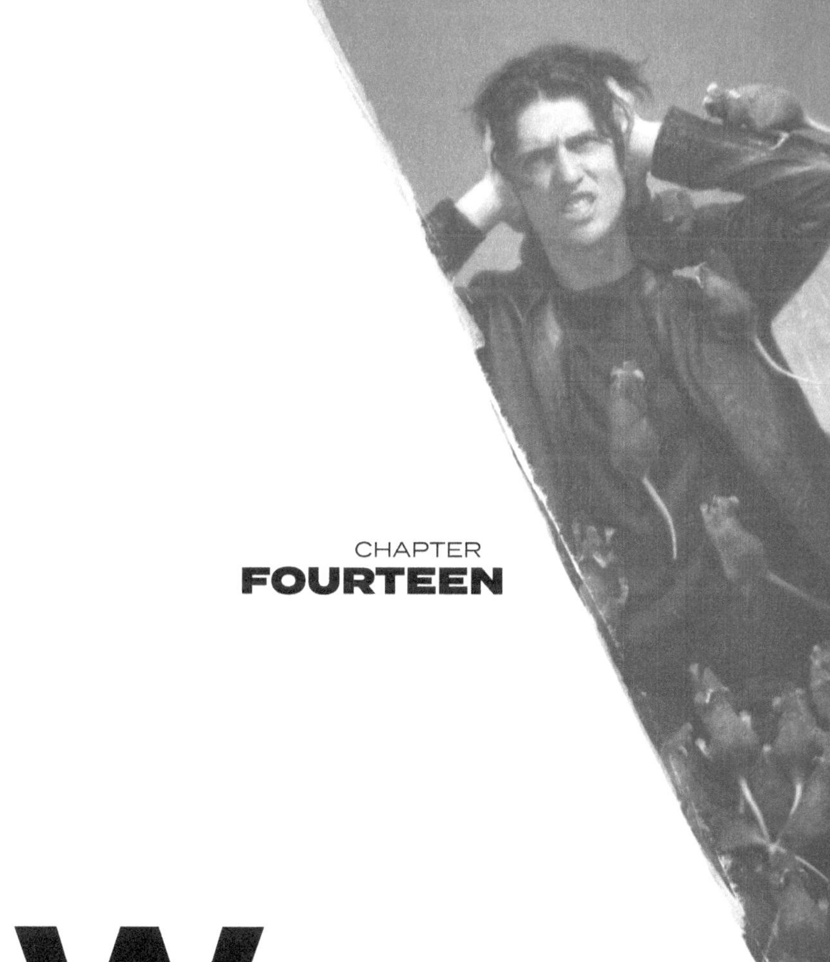

W E MADE OUR way back through the dark tunnels in relative silence. Harmony continued to sniffle as she followed us but otherwise made no comment. I could only imagine how hard it had to be, trying to get a grip on reality after having her mind so thoroughly twisted by the Pied Piper.

I kept my eyes trained on Alex's back as we marched through the hall of rats, determined to see as few more horrors today as possible. The things I had just survived would be with me for a lifetime, I knew.

But despite the horrors we'd just been through, there was a pep in my step that wouldn't go away as we marched through the mud. My soul, if it was still actually in my body—for all I knew it was in some sort of escrow holding until my contract was up—felt lighter.

We'd helped someone. Actually, if I understood the level of Clarissa's plan, we might have helped *everyone*. But at the very least, we had saved Harmony. Twice. That felt good. The circumstances that had thrown me into this adventure might be the worst thing that ever happened to me, but today was one of the better ones.

I was beginning to realize that in losing my soul, I might have found my home.

After what felt like an eternity, we came out of the depths of the tunnel abyss into the LA River, where Lazarus and his tactical squad were waiting. The old man was sitting in a lawn chair, sipping from a cocktail, when we emerged, and he raised it in a cheery salute.

"I see the hunt was successful?" he called.

"Clarissa is dead," Orion agreed, tone emotionless.

"Then our alliance has run its course." His guards shifted, postures becoming more rigid.

"It has." Orion couldn't have been more unbothered by the dozen junior Nephilim surrounding us.

"And what of my property? I can't help but notice that you're rather empty-handed."

"There was a fire," I told him with an offhanded shrug. "It got out of control." Lazarus eyed us coldly over the top of his drink before setting it down without taking a sip.

"I can't help but notice that you are the only one who have benefited from this partnership, Hunter." His voice was dark. "It's enough to make a man feel cheated."

"Send your men into the tunnels, Lazarus," Orion scoffed, turning away from the man and walking away. None of the mobster's guards made a move to stop us. "See what was waiting in the dark and tell yourself that any of your men could have killed it. An Immortal stole from you, and now she is dead. You gain plenty."

A sneer crossed over Lazarus's face, but he nodded, and his men filed into the storm drain we had just exited, following our path. I felt a grim smile grow on my face as I imagined their expressions when they saw the corpse of the scorpion lying in the depths.

This was what it meant to be an acolyte of the Hunter. A faint ember of hope began to grow in my heart as I followed my Nephilim friends to the van, stepping around a pair of dandelions that had bloomed in a crack of the river's cement. A problem for another day. Maybe my life wasn't going to end how I wanted, but it was certainly shaping up to be a life worth living.

REVIEWS

We did it! We made it to the end of the story. I hoped you enjoyed reading *Piper's Price* as much as I did writing it. If you did, the best way to help me spread the word is by leaving a review! Millions of books are published on Amazon every year. The best way to get traction and discoverability is through the reviews that readers leave. So if you enjoyed it, please let people know!

If this was your first time reading anything in The Debt Collection universe, I have good news! There's more! Matt's journey beings with *SOUL FRAUD* which you can on Amazon or by scanning this QR code.

See you soon,

Andrew

PATREON

If you're unfamiliar, Patreon is a place where you can support your favorite authors and get access to books while they are still being worked on. You can get everything from my sincere thanks to a chance to give me feedback on the direction of the story. You can subscribe for a day, a month, or a year. It is not required by any means, but it does help me to continue this adventure!

To read the next book of the Debt Collection, *SLEEP DEBT*, early, as well as my other writing projects, use the link to the Patreon below or scan the QR code with your phone.

www.patreon.com/AndrewGivler